CARLY SMITH

When the Paint Dries

First edition

ISBN: 979-8-9931709-0-9

Cover art by Trista Oberle
Editing by Hilary Rezmerski
Editing by Hayley Smith

This book was professionally typeset on Reedsy.
Find out more at reedsy.com

For my family, for believing in me and encouraging me to follow my dreams.

Contents

Preface

Content Warning

This book contains themes that may be distressing to some readers, including self-harm, depression, domestic violence, and other sensitive mental health topics. Reader discretion is advised.

If you or someone you love is struggling, please know that you are not alone. Help is available. You can call or text the Suicide & Crisis Lifeline at **988** for free, 24/7, confidential support.

Your mental health matters, and there is always hope. Please take care of yourself while reading.

Acknowledgments

To my family- thank you for your constant love and encouragement, for believing in me when I struggled to believe in myself.

To my boyfriend- thank you for letting me write in your room for hours on end without complaint, knowing how much it meant to me.

To my friends- the ones who listened to me ramble about ideas I had, or constantly told me how excited you were to read it- you mean more to me than you know.

To the readers who picked up this book- thank you for giving my characters a place to live outside of my head. I hope their stories stay with you.

To anyone who has ever felt lost, uncertain, broken, or struggled with their mental health- this book is for you. You're not alone, and healing is never a straight line. Keep moving forward.

1

~a blank page

My feet heavily scrape the pavement as I move my legs faster than I ever have before. I have to. A horn blares as I cross the street, not recognizing where I am. I turn wide-eyed, hoping I lost him. I didn't. He's close behind. I can feel his breath as he tries to take mine. His rough hands take hold of the back of my neck. My mouth is wide, but nothing is escaping from it. Fists clenched, I open my eyes to see the sky. The ground slips out from underneath me. As my head strikes the pavement, darkness envelopes me, swallowing me whole.

* * *

"Mom, do I really have to go?" I ask as I watch my mom pack my entire life into two measly suitcases.

"Honey, we have been over this. It is what your therapist recommended to us," she replies as I flop onto my empty bed. I watch my fan spin as she keeps talking. Nothing I could say will change their minds. Typical. What does my therapist know anyway? This is probably going to be a complete waste of time.

"Whatever, Mom." I sit up as she hands me a brochure. Who still uses brochures? ART IS THE BRIDGE TO THE MIND is plastered at the top. So that looks fake and cheesy. Awesome. My eyes roll into the back of my head as I toss the brochure onto the floor.

"I'll go, but I can't promise I'll enjoy it," I tell my mom.

"You know, I understand. We just want you to get better, baby. Plus, you'll get to live in your own apartment, which you don't even have to pay for," she grins.

"Awesome," I say with a fake smile. I'm not even good at art. How could it possibly help me? My eyes connect with the bruise on my leg, and the pain from my cut lip evolves. Forget this, I don't even need help.

I throw some sweats into the suitcase as my mom pulled my favorite green dress out of my closet. "What about this, honey?" she says.

I cross my arms across my chest. "What would I possibly need that for? Sitting in my room by myself?" I roll my eyes.

"You never know! Maybe you'll meet some friends you want to have dinner with or something," she says as she throws it into my suitcase. I nod my head slowly, and she smiles at me.

"Alright, let's finish up so we can get on the road. I snatch my backpack off the ground and double-check that my stuffed tiger is still in there. I know I am almost 21, but I need it. Especially living 3 hours away. I love my small Vermont town, but nothing could ever change what happened here. Maybe a change of scenery would help me forget. What am I thinking? It's burned into my brain.

* * *

Before I know it, a speed bump jolts me awake, then another. I open my eyes as a large, rustic building emerges from behind some trees. Fall is my favorite season, but this year, I'm having a hard time enjoying it. Maybe it's because my parents are shipping me off.

My dad shifts the car into park, and I plop my head into my hands.

"You will have a great time, Buggy, I know you will," my dad says as he turns around to look at me. He's called me Buggy since I was a little kid because of my huge blue eyes that pop out at you whenever you look at me.

"I'll be the judge of that," I say as I hop out of the car and look around. It is very depressing here. I glance at what they said is the campus. Not sure if it can be considered a campus when there are only two buildings.

"So, where is my apartment?" I say softly.

"I think it's just down the street, we'll find it after we check you in," my dad responds. My head falls back, and I trail close behind them.

My parents walking me into this trap feels like I am getting dropped off at a mental hospital. I'm not damaged goods. Although sometimes they treat me as if I am.

"Checking in, Sadie Harper," my mom says with a smile. Now it really feels like I'm being checked into a mental hospital.

"She is all checked in," the front desk lady replies. She hands me a packet with a schedule in it.

"Thanks," I reply and grab the packet. Her smile is a little too fake, in my opinion. I make my way back to the car with my head down. I'm not really interested in making friends here.

"Okay, Sades, let's head to your apartment," my mom says as she runs to catch up with me. My apartment isn't far, but

3

it doesn't look appealing from the outside. The inside seems more livable. We haul my things up the stairs like we did my first year of college. This time feels different. After finding room 210, I set my stuff down in the bedroom and collapse onto the floor. I am exhausted, and we haven't even started yet.

"Oh, Sadie, honey, I promise it will be okay. We will come to visit any time you want us to," my dad says as he heads toward me.

"Thanks, Dad. I think I need a nap," I respond.

"Well, just remember you have orientation in an hour, so let's get some of your room set up before," my mom chimes in from the kitchen. I groan as I sit up and look around my room. The view from my window is pretty enough to distract me from the torture I'm about to endure.

* * *

Before I knew it, 5:00 hit. I grab my purse and say bye to my parents before they head back to Vermont. My life in Vermont was always easy, comforting even. I haven't even had the chance to finish college. That's where everyone starts their new life. But who knows? Maybe I'll start a new life here, in New Haven, Connecticut, away from everything that sent me here in the first place. I walk into the same building as I had earlier that day and follow a couple of other 20-something-year-olds to a room covered, and I mean covered, in paintings. I seriously don't know how this is supposed to help me when I can only draw stick figures. I find an empty table and sit down. My bag is in front of me on the table. The teacher, or whatever you would call her, stops in front of me and smiles.

4

"Hi, you must be Sadie. I'm Clara, the instructor for this program. We are so glad you are here," she says. She seems genuine, I guess. I don't know who is real and who is fake anymore, honestly.

"Hi, it's nice to meet you," I respond. She hands me a blank piece of paper and goes back to the front of the room.

"Alright, I believe I have met most of you by now, so let's just get right into it. This isn't like school or an art class that you are being forced to take. You have all the freedom you want here. Anything you need, we will provide for you," she says loudly for everyone else to hear. Now I really feel like I'm in a mental hospital.

"This is a 4-month-long program with the possibility of it being longer if you need it. But I hope that by the end of the four months, you won't. Every day, you will be here from 2:00 to 6:00, with dinner options available afterwards. I know this may be foreign territory to some of you, but if you lean into it, I promise you will benefit from it," she says with a smile.

She finishes handing out blank pieces of paper. I didn't know I had to start this right away. I grab a pen from the bin as she explains that there are no rules. To just draw whatever we were feeling. The joke's on her, I'm hardly feeling anything. There honestly aren't many people here. Maybe 20 people my age or older. I was afraid it would just be immature young kids. But I'm right about one thing. Just a room full of damaged kids like me, shipped off to be fixed. There's a girl near me with long black hair and glasses. I think she sensed I was staring at her because she turns toward me and smiles. I smile back. Not a big smile with my teeth or anything. Just a smile you give when you pass an old friend in the hallway at school.

I stare at my mostly blank paper. Nothing but my name and

a squiggle in the corner.

"You look like you could use a friend," a gentle voice says behind me. I turn around and lock eyes with a boy with chestnut hair. He spoke softly, glancing at my paper.

"If it makes this place more bearable, then I can't disagree," I whisper back. He smiles and looks back at me.

"I'm Derek," he says slowly.

"Sadie," I say, and extend my hand to shake his. His fingers linger on mine as he looks down at the scarring on my hands. I pull my hand away and glance back down at my paper. He sets his belongings down on the spot next to me.

"I don't know what to draw either, this isn't exactly my cup of tea," he says quietly. I laugh, and so did he. He seems nice, but like I said, I'm not here to make friends. I start to draw a unicorn because, honestly, that's all I remember from elementary school art classes. I don't find this very therapeutic.

"Okay, everyone, your big project will be a partner mural that you will work on for the duration of the program. So, please find a partner," Clara says to all of us. Oh crap, I know exactly where this is about to go.

"So, do you want to be my partner? That unicorn is top of the line drawing," Derek says, turning his whole body to me. Well, I guess I don't have a choice, considering I literally know no one else.

"Yeah, sure," I reply. He nods and continues with his drawing.

* * *

My unicorn looks mid, and feeling discouraged is an understatement. This is supposed to make me feel better, not like garbage. I plop my head into my hands.

"Hey, don't worry if it isn't great. It's more about the process… I think," Derek says as he looks at my unicorn.

"Yeah, your house isn't much better," I say and laugh quietly.

"Got me there," he chuckles and rips another piece of paper out of his notebook. "Why don't you give me your number so we can make plans for the mural?" he says as he gets up and hands me the ripped-out sheet.

"Sure," I write my number on the small sheet of paper and hand it back to him.

"Cool, I'll text you later," he responds. He slips the paper in his pocket, like it's worth something to him.

"Only if it's about Mural stuff," I say with a small smile. Hardly looking up at him.

"Yes, strictly professional," he responds, grinning wider than I am. I roll my eyes, still smiling as he leaves the room.

I walk around the building a little bit before leaving. Maybe there is a good place for me to sit and write. I find this little corner with a couple of cute seats, and I will definitely be coming here to write this week. I head back down to the lobby to go back to my apartment and see Derek sitting outside on the bench. I don't know if I should pretend I don't see him, or say something. Social situations aren't really my thing recently.

"Sadie, wait up," I hear Derek's gentle voice behind me. I guess I have to talk to him. I turn around and see him jogging to catch up to me. My eyes drift down to his one leg that's stiffer than the other as he limps toward me. I smile at him, and I hope he'll keep this short.

"Hey, were you waiting for me?" I ask.

"Yeah, um, I was just wondering if you maybe want to grab coffee or something and talk about the mural?" he asks

7

hesitantly. "There's a coffee shop down the road, I found," he continues. I freeze for a second as I move my wandering eyes up to his eyes that are way above mine. He is at least a head taller than I am. I study his brown eyes, then look back down at my feet.

"Um, maybe tomorrow, I have some unpacking to do, sorry," I say.

"Oh yeah, no worries, I'll catch you tomorrow," he responds. He sounds a little disappointed. But like I said, I'm not here to get a boyfriend or make friends. Just to make my parents and therapist happy. I turn and continue my way out the door and toward my apartment, which you can see from the building. As I walk, I feel him still close behind me. My heart rate increases, and I start to walk faster. I glance back to see him behind me, and we lock eyes. I pick up my pace. What if his niceness is just a mask? I buzz into the apartment complex and slip in through the door as it shuts quickly behind me, but not before he can grab the door to sneak in too. I should say something. I should ask for help.

I turn around to face him and firmly say, "What are you doing?"

"Oh, hey, Sadie, you're in this apartment too?" he says from across the lobby.

"You live here?" I question.

"Yeah, I'm pretty sure they put the majority of us in here since it's so close to the building," he says, putting his phone in his pocket. Well, that makes a little more sense. I sigh and fumble around for my key.

"Hey, are you okay?" he says as he makes his way to me.

"Yeah, yeah, I'm good, just a little overwhelmed," I reply.

"Yeah, I get it, it's quite the change," he says. He makes a lot of eye contact. It's kind of charming.

"Yeah, um, I just need to get back to my room," I say.

"Okay, yeah, well, I'll see you tomorrow," he says with a smile. I smile, and it quickly fades as I turn to take the stairs.

"Um, Sadie, one more thing, I'm in room 306 if you need anything, okay?" he whispers.

"Okay, yeah, thanks, I'm in 210," I say quietly as I turn to walk away.

2

~something like a tree

I get up early most days. Not really by choice, but more that when the sun comes up, my body wakes me up. My mom got me an espresso machine out of pity for sending me here. Lucky for her, bribes work well on me. They also got me a ton of groceries and snacks, so I wouldn't have to worry about that yet, which is nice. I make myself a latte and sit on the floor of my balcony with my favorite blanket and watch the sun continue to rise above the trees.

My apartment faces the art building, but I can see practically down the street both ways. A cute, rustic coffee shop to the right and a 1950s-themed diner to the left. Guess this town can't pick a theme.

When I was in high school, I loved to write. I thought for sure I would go to college and get an English or writing degree or something. Now my dreams are just dreams. But that doesn't stop me from doing it every once in a while with a latte in hand.

* * *

I put on my comfort sweat set and grab my bag before heading over to the building. As I shut the apartment door behind me, my phone starts to buzz in my pocket.

INCOMING: Jules.

Finally, I was starting to think she'd never call me.

"Helloooo, it's about time you called me," I say into my phone.

"Haha soooo funny. How's the move-in going thus far?" she asks.

"You know fine, I guess. It's kind of nice to fulfill my dream of living in an apartment with a balcony," I say.

Julia laughs. "I'm so glad. What are you doing right now?" she asks.

"Just heading to the program. It's 2-6 every day, so don't call me during that time," I say.

"Yep, don't you worry, that's when I have Soccer anyway. We can plan on talking every other day, after, okay?" she says.

"I would love that," I reply. "Well, I'm almost there. It's like a 90-second walk, so I gotta go, but we'll talk later. Love ya," I say with a smile.

"I hope it's good today. Love you too," she replies. I hang up the phone just as I'm about to enter the building. I miss Julia. We've been friends since childhood. We fell out of touch every so often, but we were attached at the hip come high school. A lot of my other friends stopped talking to me after everything happened, so sometimes it feels like Julia is the only one I really have left from home.

The room is half full, and Derek is already sitting at the same table as yesterday. His brown long-sleeve shirt runs past his wrists and is tucked into some dark-wash jeans. I quickly walk by, hoping he wouldn't notice, but of course, he did.

"Heyyy, Sadie, you made it. How's it going?" he asks.

11

"Um, I'm good, how about you?" I ask with a soft smile.

"I'm pretty good-" he replies, but gets cut off by instructor Clara telling us to get together with our partners. She also says that we each will get our own little room to work on the murals. I get up and follow Derek into one of the little rooms. The sun filters in through the tall windows on one side and a giant canvas on the other.

"Wow, this is legit," he murmurs as he walks around the room.

I look around. "Yeah, it's cool, I guess," I say. Clara brings in a large bucket of supplies for our use, and she sets it on the table.

"You two do not need to use the whole time today. Just get an idea for what you want to do and sketch it up. Good luck!" Clara exclaims.

"Okayyy then, do you have any brilliant ideas?" I ask Derek. He sets his stuff down and stares at the supplies on the table.

"Do you um, like trees?" he asks. I giggle and look back at him from the giant canvas.

"Trees?" I repeat.

"Yeah, like something about starting from the ground up... growth and all that deep metaphor crap," he shrugs.

"I suppose trees are alright," I say as I continue to laugh. A real laugh. He chuckles and looks around the room.

"I say we just start with a pencil drawing of a tree and see where that takes us?"

"Yeah, sure, I think that could be good," I grab a pencil and a sheet of paper. As we work on the sketch of a tree, I wonder why he's here. I know I shouldn't judge a book by its cover, but I can't stop my mind from running through a list of reasons why he's in the program. He doesn't seem like the kind of person who'd need art therapy. Whatever that kind of person is. Maybe it's grief. Maybe depression. Maybe something no one saw. I catch myself almost judging, then I look back at my own life. Who am I to assume?

Our tree is tall and kind of crooked. Awkward even. I feel like this could take us somewhere, I think.

"Honestly, this idea is eating," he says as he backs away a little bit.

"You know I think you're right," I reply quietly. We sit in silence for a while, checking our phones or doodling ideas in our notebooks.

"Sooooo," he starts, not looking up at me. "Where are you from?" he asks hesitantly.

"Small town in Vermont. I love it there," I say. "What about you?" I ask, still tracing the outline for the trunk.

"Suburb outside Boston, and I don't love it there," he laughs.

"Why not?"

"I don't know, it's boring. Nothing for me there," he finishes and looks up at me.

"Oh."

"What's Vermont like?" he asks.

I smile a little, "Green. Calm. Quiet. It's the kind of place where people know your name even if they've never talked to you."

"Sounds peaceful," he says.

"It is," I say. "But it can feel small sometimes, you know? But I think part of me likes it like that." he nods, like he gets it. "It made the world feel manageable. Like anything I wanted was within my grasp."

He leans back and looks into my eyes. "Yeah. I think I'm the opposite. I want things to feel big. Like, there's more out there than just what I know."

"There is," I say.

He smiles. "You sure?"

I nod. "Pretty sure."

"Maybe that's why I am partly glad that I'm here. Get to see new things," he says.

I nod in agreement and play around with my pencil. "I like to travel. I've lived in New England my whole life, but I've never been to New York," I say quietly.

He leans back and brushes his hair out of his face. "Really?" he responds. I nod and look down. "I went with some friends in high school. Lots of trash and people. So honestly, you're not missing much."

I smile. "See, everyone says that, but I think it's more than that. I want to see Times Square in the middle of the night, walk in Central Park, or try a street hot dog," I say, looking back at him.

"Mm, I gotcha," he responds, eyes drifting back to the drawing.

He tilts his head slightly, watching my pencil move up the tree trunk. I feel like I've traced over this line a thousand times.

* * *

I grab my bike from the rack outside the apartment complex and pedal down to the grocery store to grab a couple of things. I like almond milk for my lattes and fruity tea with honey. Essentials for living on my own. I spot a giant watermelon I need, but it definitely won't fit in my bike basket. So, I guess I will have to come back for it. I spot myself in the self-checkout mirror, and my eyes are drawn to my grown-out highlights. I should've thought about that before coming here.

I spot a girl around my age perched on the bench outside the store. "Excuse me, do you know if there's a hair salon around here somewhere?" I ask her timidly.

She looks up and smiles at me. "Yes, there's one a couple of miles away called Elan Studio," she responds.

I smile and nod. "Okay, thank you," I say as I unlock my bike from the rack. I go online quickly and make an appointment for next week. Might as well treat myself while I'm here.

* * *

I enjoy my blueberry pomegranate tea with honey on my couch, watching my comfort movie, *The Kissing Booth.* It's quiet in this town. Reminds me of home in that way.

The tea is warm in my hands, the movie is familiar, and for a little while, it feels like nothing is urgent. Like everything can move at my pace. Outside, the wind taps lightly against the window, like it knows not to interrupt me.

I don't mind being alone sometimes. I think I was made for these moments. The still ones, when the world slows down and I can breathe without having to explain why or pretend to be something I'm not.

3

~quiet lines

I have been thinking about doing something new with my hair for a while. I've always kept it long, but maybe a new city deserves a new version of me. Partial foil to brighten up my roots and five inches cut off.

I walk out of the salon feeling refreshed and like a different person. My hair catches the afternoon light, warmer and softer around my face. People say hair holds memories, which gives me even more of a reason to make a change. I glance at my reflection in a car window. She's still me, just a little softer and fuller of life.

* * *

I hate being unproductive. Nothing is worse than the fatigue and boredom that come with it. There's not much for me to do here. I need to find a hobby or something. I need something else to do besides this. I decide to show up early to our room since I was bored, and I want to start brainstorming things for our tree.

"What's up, Sadie? How are ya?" Derek says as he enters our room and plops down on the stool next to me.

"I'm good, you?"

"Not too bad, I definitely think we should start on our big sketch today," he says, setting his stuff down. I nod and grab a pencil from our tray.

"I'm nervous," I blurt out, shaking my legs up and down.

"It's just a pencil, it'll be fine," he says calmly.

"Okay, okay, start with the trunk?" I ask.

"Let's do it."

I pull out a picture for inspiration on my phone and show it to him. "Looks great, I like how there's a lot of branches and roots," he says. He squats at the bottom of the canvas and starts to draw the roots. I follow the base of the trunk and trace it upward.

"What did you do this morning?" he asks, not moving his eyes away from the canvas.

How do I say I sat on my couch without sounding like a bore? "Umm, got my hair done," I smile and push all my hair behind my shoulders.

"Looks nice," he says, trying not to smile.

"Thanks," I say, playing with the front piece of my hair.

We work in silence once more. The roots are good, and the outline is starting to come to life.

"Sooo..." I say, trying to break the silence that is making my skin itch. "What's your story, Derek?" I ask.

He lets out a dramatic gasp as if I just insulted him. "You can't just ask someone what their trauma is, Sadie," he says mid-laugh.

I smile. "I know, I know, but maybe if we get to know each other better, the mural won't look so much like two strangers

17

painted it," I suggest.

He shrugs, and he stops laughing. "I suppose." He pops up from his squat and sits down near his things. He takes a breath before moving to grab his bag and twists around a red tag hanging from it that says *Ohio State* on it. His joking energy slips away. "I got recruited to play football for them in high school. I had an amazing freshman season. Scored fourteen touchdowns." I nod in response, but I think there's more coming.

"Well, toward the end of the season, I collided with a 300-pound linebacker and blew out my knee," he says hesitantly. My smile fades as I continue to lock eyes with him.

"Oh," I say quietly. "I'm really sorry," I stutter as he looks away from me and back to his tag.

He takes a deep breath, "Tore my ACL completely and part of my meniscus. Surgery didn't go great, and they told me I would never run the same. They said it was wise if I medically retired," he continues. A heavy silence falls between us. I don't think there's really anything I could say. "And well, after that, I kind of got in with a bad crowd. One thing led to another, and I sort of crashed out. Parents freaked, and now here I am," he says slowly. He sits up straight and smiles at me.

"But, I'm good, you know. Just the way life goes. Gotta see this through for my sister though." he says. He has a sister. I make a note of that.

My mouth opens slightly before I ask, "How old is your sister?"

"14," he responds. "Yeah, I would do anything for her, ya know. She was really scared, and that scared me right out of the shenanigans I was doing," he lets out a short laugh that almost seems forced. He's protective of his sister. It's refreshing to see someone care that much about their younger sibling.

My brother wouldn't know what that looks like.

I pause, "Yeah, I get that. Well, I'm glad you're doing better. And now you'll be good at art?" I say with the corners of my mouth turning up. He laughs and sets his bag back on the ground.

"I suppose you're right," he says with a smile. "So Sadie…" he grabs my bag that has my full name on it, "Jean Harper, that has a nice ring to it," he says, flashing his bright white teeth at me. "So Sadie Jean Harper, what's *your* story?" he continues.

I freeze. I stammer to get any words out. "I um- I" before I could completely embarrass myself, Clara pokes her head into our room.

"We're nearing the end today, so if you guys would clean up a little before you head out, that would be awesome! I'll see you both tomorrow," she says. I jump up to start grabbing supplies, hoping he had forgotten what he had asked.

"Sounds good," he replies to Clara and starts to grab our utensils to put back. All we have on our canvas is a trunk that may be the start of something. He turns to smile at me as he grabs his things to leave.

"See you tomorrow," he says. "Sadie Jean. Have a good night," he finishes and brushes his hair out of the way of his eyes.

"Yeah, thanks. You too." I stumble over my words. Before I even finish my sentence, he's walking out the door.

The silence comes back.

4

~unpacked

My apartment is cold and a little sad. As if it's mirroring the inside of my head. I've been procrastinating unpacking because I know that once I start, I couldn't leave, even if I tried. I ordered some things to decorate my walls with before I left home. Still smashed together in a box, I pull out some of my framed signed vinyl posters by my favorite artists, along with all 47 vinyls that I have in my possession. I hung up some miscellaneous string lights and a couple of pictures of me and Julia. I guess if I have to be here, I might as well make it look a little less like a prison cell. I flop onto my couch and feel my phone buzz in my pocket.

Maybe: Derek: *Heyyy its derek*

Oh my gosh, I forgot I gave him my number. I honestly didn't even think he'd text me. Thought he was just being nice. I roll my eyes at myself.

Am I serious? Why would I think that he wouldn't text about the project? I put my phone down while I decide if I want to respond. I pick my phone up and set it down at least four times. I have been on edge for a while now, wary of everyone around me. Maybe it's time I stop that. Julia is always telling me that not everyone is a bad person. That not everyone is out to hurt me. But sometimes, it's a little hard to believe. I pick up my phone once more and click on his text.

Me: hi *Derek*

Derek: *sooo what are you doing with your night*

I roll over onto my back and try to decide if I should tell him what I am actually doing or if I should lie to sound cooler.

Me: *still unpacking lol. decorating too*

Derek: *yeah me too. I have a lot more stuff then I realized haha*

I look at my wall covered with music posters. It's already 11:00. I'm glad I don't have to have a job while we're here. It's nice.

Me: *yeah same here lol*

Derek: *want to maybe take a break?*

Me: *this doesn't seem like professional talk only derekkk*

Derek: *oops I forgot*

Me: *okay yeah I could use a break*

Derek: *oh yeaaa*

Derek: *the diner down the street is 24 hours... Skippy's I think it's called.*

Me: *sure, lemme get changed*

Derek: *bet i'll meet you in the lobby in 10*

I set my phone down and stomp my feet against the couch. Three pairs of jeans later, and I finally land on ones that are low-rise and have several rips in them. A pink long-sleeved crop top should suffice. Is this a date? Probably not. What is wrong with me? I don't want a boyfriend, so I hope he doesn't think I said yes to a date. My hair falls from my claw clip and onto my back. My mirror says I look okay. I don't know if I believe it, though.

"There she is," I hear a faint voice behind me as I face the door of the lobby. I turn to face him. He's wearing brown cargo pants and a gray long-sleeved shirt, similar to the brown one he was wearing yesterday.

I smile without my teeth and clasp my hands together with my arms straight. "Hi," I say quietly, cocking my head to the right.

He smiles back and tucks his hands into his front pockets. "You ready?" he says. I nod, and he opens the door and motions for me to go first.

Skippy's diner smells of burnt toast and coffee. It looks like a typical diner. Red seats, old vintage vibes. It's already 11:30, so it is pretty empty here. Just a middle-aged couple in the corner holding hands and looking through the menu. Derek leans back in the booth and grabs a menu from the holder.

"I think I need some waffles, honestly," he says without looking up from the menu. "What about you? What are you getting?" he asks. My face gets hot, and I can't help but grin.

I stare at the syrup stains on the menu. Now that I'm really thinking about it, I'm not that hungry.

"I think… a latte."

"A latte at midnight… huh, interesting choice," he muses, looking up at me from the menu.

"Ha, yeah, I guess it's just like a comfort thing," I say while folding the straw wrapper. He nods slowly. "My mom and I used to make these creative lattes if we couldn't sleep sometimes," I continue. "Decaf, of course."

"Ohhh, that makes sense," he responds. "Are you close with your mom?" he asks.

I hesitate. "Yeah, we used to be really close," I say quietly.

22

"Not anymore?" he asks, sitting forward in the booth. His face is close to mine. I look into his eyes.

"Kind of?" I reply. Before he can say anything else, the waitress comes to take our order. Her apron is stained with coffee and syrup. She comes back with it quickly since it's practically empty in here.

We sit in silence for a couple of minutes while he eats his waffles. I stir my latte, vanilla with almond milk.

"Okay, let me ask you something," he breaks the silence. I draw in a sharp breath. Oh boy, I'm nervous.

"Okay…" I respond hesitantly.

"What is the biggest misconception people have about you?" he asks. I nod slowly. Okay, that was deep… how do I even respond to that? I rack my brain for possible answers.

I look at him, waiting for me to answer. "That I moved on," I say slowly, hoping he doesn't ask follow-up questions.

"What do you mean?" he questions, as any normal person would. I hesitate to say what I want to say. I don't want to scare him away.

"That just because we survived something, doesn't mean we've moved on from it. If you know what I mean," I say doubtfully.

"Ah yeah, I do get that actually," he says, looking at his empty plate.

"What about you?"

"People think I'm good at art," he smirks, trying to lighten the mood. This is good, funny.

I throw my straw wrapper at him, "Mm, no one thinks that, Derek."

"Wow," he says between laughs. He doesn't say much else. But in the moment, I forget everything. I actually feel

23

comfortable. No alarms are going off in my head. I finally feel like I'm not in danger.

"Oh, shoot, it's late," I say. He sets down his phone and places his hands on the table. That two hours went by quickly.

"Oh well, we're young," he shrugs and smiles at me. "But we can get going if you want."

I nod and grab my keys to leave and walk ahead of him. We walk back to our apartments mostly in silence. I'm exhausted. But I can't tell him that I usually don't stay up past 10:30, and that not everyone can get me out past then. Really, only Julia can, and that's on a very rare occasion when I need to sober cab her and her older boyfriend.

He walks me to my room even though it's not on the same floor as his. My keys clatter as I attempt to open my door, but my hands shake a little. I look at him and look down as I finally get the door unlocked.

"Well, um, thanks for tonight, it was a much-needed break," I say and softly smile.

"Of course, anytime," he says, smiling too. "Goodnight, Sadie," he continues as he inches away without losing eye contact.

"Goodnight, Derek," I say as I step into my room and shut the door behind me.

5

~in passing

After a couple of weeks of working on our mural, we haven't made very much progress. For a while, we were afraid to paint in case we messed up, but I finally think we're ready to start painting. Our outline of our tree seems to be done. I hope.

Derek and I haven't talked a lot in those couple of weeks. His parents came into town for a while, and he was busy. But I am actually enjoying getting to know him. He's very kind and down to Earth. One night, I may or may not have stalked his football highlights. He was really good, but more importantly, he looked so happy being out on that field.

I love the beginning of October. The weather makes me feel all warm inside, and the pumpkins remind me of home.

I find my little corner of the art building and sit with my pumpkin latte and my notebook. A couple of years ago, I started messing around with writing song lyrics. It kind of just came naturally, but I gave up on it after everything. Now that I've been here for almost a month, I want to get back to doing things I enjoy.

I check the time and realize I'm late. I snatch my things off the ground and hustle down the stairs.

"You ready to start painting?" Derek asks as I burst into our room. Our tree outline stares me down.

"Let's hope so," I reply. He turns to face me, and I try and catch my breath. "Are we just going to do the trunk today?"

"Yeah, let's do that," he says. "Remember this is supposed to be messy, that's the point. It doesn't need to be perfect in the slightest," he continues. The type A in me is fighting for its life right now. Because doesn't everything need to be perfect? Or at least try to be?

"Yep, sounds good, I'll do my best," I say quietly. He smiles and turns to pour the different browns into our tray. I start with the bottom, and he goes more toward the middle. The variety is important, he reminds me several times, to show our different perspectives. I'm starting to think this isn't so bad. It is calming. Derek lets me pick what we listen to, which is usually indie music. Turns out we have pretty similar tastes in music.

I'm starting with a medium brown, almost the color of Derek's hair. I step back to double-check that what I've just painted doesn't look horrible. Derek says we need to take it nice and slow since we have like three more months for this mural. I look up at Derek on a stool, working on the middle of the trunk.

His long sleeves fall from his wrists to his elbows, exposing his horizontal scars. I stare at them. I'm taken aback. I had no idea. My eyes linger longer than they should. I tell myself to look away, but I can't. They don't look very recent, but they don't look very old either. He turns around to look at me, as if he notices me staring. I quickly look back down at my

26

section and clear my throat. He tugs his sleeves back down to his wrists. I want to say something, anything, but nothing seems right.

I mix my brown more with my brush and say, "I like this shade, I think it's perfect for the bottom. It's warm." He nods from his stool without looking away from his brush. His posture softens a little, and we don't talk much now while we're working. The room seems tense now, and I wonder if I'm the only one who notices.

"Hey, um, I think I'm gonna head out if that's okay," I announce quietly, not looking up to see him.

"We still have a good hour left to work. Is everything okay?" he asks as he hops down from the stool to face me. He stands inches away from me. He takes a step toward me, and I take a step back and tuck the front pieces of my hair behind my ears.

"Yeah, I just need to go," I say as I grab my bag and quickly leave the room.

"Sadie, wait," I hear him faintly, and I hear his footsteps behind me, but they stop outside the room. I run all the way back to my apartment.

* * *

I flop on my couch and glance at my vinyls. I jump up to put on my favorite album. *For Emma* by Bon Iver. It calms me. Brings me back to earth when I feel like I'm floating. The record player crackles a bit when I place the needle on.

Back onto the couch I go.

I lost a lot of my friends last year. Turns out, when you're being manipulated, you stop prioritizing those who actually mean something to you. A lot of people won't put up with that.

I don't blame them. They didn't know. Only Julia stuck by me, and I'm grateful. She loves me. Even when I don't love myself.

Jules: *missing you rn ughhh*

I smile and turn on my side to respond.

Me: *i miss you too*

Listening to our fav album rn

Jules: *for emma!*

Me: *the best*

Jules: *ill listen rn too*

Me: *yes do it*

I set my phone down and turn my record player up. It crackles a bit more, but I don't mind. I think it sounds better that way sometimes. Makes it feel more real.

The lyrics fill my room. It seems raw, quiet, and aching in a way that makes me feel understood. I close my eyes and let the music settle around me. For a moment, it's just me, Bon Iver, and the soft glow of the street lights bleeding through the curtains.

I think about our tree. About the shade of brown I chose. About the way Derek tugged at his sleeves and how I couldn't find the right words to say. I feel unsettled. Like maybe I could've said something to help. I don't think he knows what I saw, though.

Another unproductive day has struck again. My therapist says to use this time to engage in mindful activities. But I don't have the energy.

Maybe tomorrow, I'll try again.

6

~for now

My balcony has quickly become my new favorite place. I went to the store and got a cute, comfy chair to put out there so I can read or write in the mornings. I also brought out the coffee table from inside, so I'd have a place to put my lattes. I'm writing new lyrics. I don't sing well, but it helps to put my feelings into words. I spoke to my therapist last week. I told her I made a new friend and that I was actually starting to enjoy painting. Was that entirely true? I'm not sure, but it keeps her and my parents off my back for a while.

My phone buzzes on my lap as I pick up my pen.

Derek: *good morninggggg*

Me: *good morning derek*

Derek: *meet me at my room before we head over today?*

Me: *sure but why?*

Derek: *got something for ya*

I tilt my head to the left and shut my phone back off. That makes me a little bit nervous. I have zero idea what he has for me.

29

INCOMING: MOM

"Hi, Mom," I say into the phone, setting my notebook down.

"Happy birthday to youuuuu," she sings. I try to interrupt her, but she just keeps singing until the song is finished.

"Thank you, Mom, I love you," I giggle softly.

"Got anything fun planned for today?" she asks.

"Not really, just working on our project," I say.

"Oh well, your gift should be delivered by the end of the day, honey," she reassures.

"Okay, thanks, Mom. I'll let you know when I get it," I say, but my voice trails off.

"Alright, well, have a good day, okay?" she finishes.

"I will, I love you."

"I love you more," she says as I pull the phone away from my ear.

I hang up and take a deep breath. I look around at the fall colors and pull my notebook up to continue what I was writing.

* * *

I bought myself a cute sweater that I told myself I'd wear on my birthday, no matter what I was doing. It's brown and has beige stripes. Perfect for this time of year, I think. I head up to Derek's room, still unsure of what he has for me. I knock and wait for him to answer. The door whips open, and there he is with a bouquet in his hand.

"Happy birthday, Sadie," he says with a huge smile on his face.

"How in the world did you know it's my birthday?" I ask incredulously, stepping into his apartment for the first time.

He shrugs, "I have my ways." He winks and motions me

toward his island that has a pile of candy and an iced latte perched next to it.

I smile at him, "Thank you, Derek, this is really nice," I say gratefully, picking up the latte and sipping from the straw. "And this is gas," I continue. He laughs and walks around to the other side of the island. "Oh my gosh, you have a guitar?" I say as I spot it perched in the corner.

"Umm, yeah, do you play?"

"Sometimes," I say, grabbing it off its stand.

"Whoa now, careful," he says jokingly.

"Yeah, yeah," I pick up and start to strum. "Let me see what you got," I hand him the guitar. He nods and takes it from my grasp. He starts to play a cute little tune, and I pull out some lyrics on my phone. "Mind if I sing some of my lyrics?" I ask.

"Um, definitely, let's hear them," he replies, strumming the guitar louder.

I pull out my phone and start harmonizing with his strumming. I hesitate before I begin to sing slowly.

"I packed my fears in folded pages, left my name in Vermont dust."

"Three hours down the line to maybe find someone I used to trust." I pause and look up at him, and we lock eyes.

"'Keep going," he whispers, not looking away from me.

A deep breath escapes my lungs. "And I don't know who I am without the weight you left behind. But every night I spend alone feels a little more like mine." I finish, and don't look up from my phone. He stops strumming.

"Sorry, that was a little dark," I say quietly, looking at his guitar.

"Don't apologize. I loved it," he says, setting his guitar down to his right side. "I didn't know we had that in common," he continues.

I shrug and smile at him. "Let me drop this off in my room before we get to work," I say, picking up the candy and flowers.

"Bet, let's do it, birthday girl," he says and opens the door for me.

I open my door and set it all down on the counter, and grab a small mason jar for the flowers. He follows me into my room and wanders around while I fill up the vase. "Alright, let's go before Clara gets mad we're late... again," I say, grabbing my bag. My Doc Martens click under me as I walk. He nods and opens the door for me once more.

* * *

"I like how it's coming along," Derek says. We started at the top of the tree. A lot of green. It's just an outline so far, though. Doesn't look like it has a voice yet.

"Me too," I say as I step back to look at it. "I'm glad it's Friday, though. I need a break from this to be honest with you," I say.

"You're not wrong about that one," he says. Stepping down from his stool. "Any plans tonight for your big day?" he asks.

"Not really, probably just going to watch a movie," I respond, sitting on the ground and looking up at him, smiling.

"Want me to join? I can cook something up."

"Yeah, sure, sounds great," I respond, looking down at my shoes. We clean up our supplies, looking at our minimal progress for today. We walk out of the building talking about a new movie that's coming out soon.

"Hey, Sades over here," I hear in the distance. I look to my left and see my parents walking toward us. My face erupts with a smile, and I run toward them.

"What are you guys doing here?" I say hugging both of them.

"Couldn't let you celebrate your birthday without us, buggy," my dad says, twisting me back and forth in a hug.

"Buggy, huh." Derek tilts his head. "That's cute, Sades," He continues, eye lingering on me.

I bite my lip, trying to hide my smile as I blush. "Derek, this is my mom and dad. Mom and Dad, this is my project partner, Derek," I say with a smile.

"Nice to meet you," Derek says and shakes both of their hands.

"Yes, you too," my mom says.

"Want to get dinner?" my dad asks. I nod, and he puts his arm around me and guides me to the car.

"Rain check on the movie?"

He nods. "Yeah, no problem."

"Okay, perfect. I'll catch you later, D," I respond, looking back at him. He nods and turns away. We laugh and walk to my parents' car.

The restaurant is cozy and dim with string lights. It's soft music, and the smell of bread that makes me realize how hungry I actually am. I sit across from my parents in a booth, still wearing my perfect birthday sweater.

They tell me about their drive up, my dad's obsession with podcasts, and my mom's eternal search for a new audiobook narrator she doesn't absolutely hate. Somewhere between appetizers and our food arriving, my mom leans in a little.

"So... tell us about this Derek," she says, raising her eyebrows.

I sip my water before answering. "He's just my project partner, Mom. We're friends. It's uncomplicated." I respond.

My dad looks at me, confused. "Uncomplicated, huh?"

I smile and nod my head yes. "We paint. We talk. He's cool.

33

It's nice having someone around who doesn't know my past." I say while moving my food around with my fork.

They nod like they're satisfied with that answer, but I think they're trying not to say too much.

I cut into my food, and for a second, I feel a little more normal. Just having dinner with my parents like we used to. No weight in my chest, no confusion. Just dinner with the two people who know me best and love me for who I am.

"Uncomplicated can be good, Sadie," my mom says finally, buttering a roll.

"Sometimes that's exactly what you need," my dad adds.

I smile. Yeah. Maybe it is.

7

~after hours

"Sorry, we didn't get dinner last night," I murmur while packing up our brushes. We didn't get much done again today. Both of us were tired and felt unmotivated. We only worked on our mural for a little bit before deciding to head out.

"Don't sweat it," he says with a smile.

I nod slowly, "Movie tonight?" I ask hesitantly.

"Some of my friends from college wanted to play video games tonight, sorry."

Oh. "Okay, yeah, no problem," I smile and pack my things quickly. "See you tomorrow then."

I can hear his mouth open, but he doesn't say anything. I just go back to my room.

I flop on my couch face up, staring at the ceiling. Throwing a stress ball up in the air to catch it again. I just sit for a while. There's nothing on my TV. I don't even go on my phone. It's on the coffee table.

My phone buzzes. I bet it's my mom checking in again, even though I just saw her. She never used to be a helicopter parent, but I guess a near-death experience will make a parent like that. So I can't even blame her. It's not my mom this time.

Derek: *hey still want to have that movie night? I got some popcorn*

Why did he change his mind?

Me: *thought you were gaming?*

Derek: *they were annoying me cant lie*

Me: *gotcha, sure come down*

Derek: *okay I'll be there in a few*

I set my phone down and run to my bathroom to wipe off the smeared mascara under my eyes and reapply. I put on a cute and flattering sweat-set. Just before I can get situated, there's a knock on my door. Oh shoot, he's here.

"Hi Derek," I say as I open the door for him.

"Well, hi there, Sades," he responds, walking past me into my apartment. My heart skips a beat whenever he calls me Sades. It's comforting coming from him. It makes me feel like someone almost understands me. He throws the popcorn into the microwave and grabs a bowl like he's lived here forever.

"So what happened to you today? You just ran out on me," he says while leaning against the counter.

"Yeah, sorry about that. I guess I just had a moment," I respond and start to walk toward my couch. The microwave beeps, and he grabs the bag and pours it into the bowl.

"Ah, okay, well let's take your mind off whatever it was with a good old Adam Sandler movie, okay?" he says as he tosses a piece into his mouth. I nod and sit down on the couch.

"Lemme use your bathroom quick before we start it," he says. I nod again. My phone buzzes on the coffee table.

INCOMING: Jules

"Hi Jules, what's up?" I say as I pick up the phone.

"Hey girl, what are you up to?"

"Um, not much. Derek came over for a movie night, kind of needed a break from painting, you know," I respond quietly, hoping he won't hear me talking about him.

"You know this could be your chance at love again," she says. I roll my eyes. Julia is always trying to set me up.

"He's a good friend, and that's what I need right now. I don't think getting into a relationship this soon is a good idea," I respond even quieter than before.

"Yeah, good point," her voice is gentle as always. I hear the door unlock, and it startles me a little bit.

"Alright, well, I'm gonna let you go so we can watch this movie," I say as Derek comes around the corner on his phone. "Talk to you later, I love ya."

"Love ya too," she says before hanging up.

He comes over and sits next to me with enough room for another person in between.

"Who was that?" he asks.

"Just Julia."

"Ahh, gotcha," he responds, flipping through my streaming services.

"Thanks for bringing the popcorn," I say, turning to look at him.

"No problem, can't have a movie without it," he responds. He starts the movie, but I'm not really watching. I glance at him. He's focused, laughing at some dumb line. And I suddenly want to say it. Just one piece of it, to someone who might understand. I turn to the TV, then back at him a few times.

"Hey, can I tell you something…?" I ask him hesitantly.

"Of course," he says, turning toward me and pausing the movie. He sits on the couch with his water in one hand and

37

the remote in the other. The popcorn bowl perched between us. "What's up?" he finishes.

"I got out of a relationship not too long before I came here," I spoke softly.

"Oh, I'm sorry, Sadie," he says. He looks disappointed.

"Yeah." I pause.

"Why did it end?" he asks.

"Well, it should've ended a while ago," I hesitate. "But when you love someone, it's hard to leave just because they're hurting you, you know?" I say slowly, looking down at my bowl of popcorn in my lap.

"Hurting you how?" he asks. I look away and eat a couple of pieces of popcorn. "Sadie?" he repeats, softer now. "Sadie… did he hurt you? Like, actually hurt you?" he asks, scooching toward me on the couch.

I shrug, "Yeah, in more ways than one," I whisper.

"Oh.." he says slowly, "are you okay?"

"Um, yeah, I'm good, let's just watch the movie," I respond. He lets out a deep breath and puts his hand on my upper arm.

"If that's all you want to tell me right now, that is totally fine, okay, Sadie? But I'm here if and when you're ready to talk more about it," he continues. I nod slowly as a tear falls from my eye. I wipe it away quickly. "Good thing Adam Sandler is funny," he says.

I laugh and say, "Good point, hit play already." He nods and starts the movie again. Movies aren't always my favorite. Maybe it's because I can't pay attention long enough. My mind is always wandering elsewhere.

The movie is just about over, and I'm kind of falling asleep. My eyes keep closing, then opening when I realize I'm dozing off.

"I know it's late, but wanna go work on our mural?" Derek says as he clicks out of the movie. I glance over at him. He looks wide awake.

"The building is locked," I stare at him.

He smirks as he reaches into his backpack. He pulls out a couple of keys on a ring. "I got them from Clara earlier."

I roll my eyes. "Fine, only for a little bit, though, okay?"

"Okayyy if you say so," he says while grabbing my arm and dragging my sleepy body off the couch. "Let's go then," he finishes. I've never stayed up late this much in my entire life. He's a bad influence on me. But honestly, I don't mind it. It's nice to have company.

* * *

He sighs as we walk into our room. "We got some work to do." I look at our tree and how little meaning there is to it. It's literally just a tree.

I nod slowly and walk toward our half tree, "No kidding," I say, not looking at him. "It needs a voice," I say while grabbing the supplies. "A voice saying something like I've been through a lot of storms, but I'm still standing. It should look weathered and tired." I continue.

"Mm, poetic, I like that. Let's get to work," he replies, smiling at me and grabbing his colors. It's midnight when we start. It's dark, the stars are out, and it's quiet, so we crack a window and let the breeze in. I add different shades of brown to the trunk and some fallen leaves around the base. I look up to see Derek doing the same, but with lighter shades. I grab my dark brown and draw a huge streak over Derek's section.

"Oh, alright, why not?" he says. It's a relief that he wasn't mad.

"Hang on, I'll blend it," I say and giggle. I start to use a clean brush to blend it in. It looks weathered. Just how I want it.

"Here, try it like this," he says as he grabs my hand. He guides my hand with the brush in a different direction. I can feel his warm breath behind me.

I quickly drop my hand. "Okay, yep, I think that's good," I say as I rush back over to the colors.

"Are you okay? I'm sorry, I was just trying to help," he responds, stepping down from his stool.

"No, it's totally fine, I'm good," I respond. "Seriously, I'm fine," I finish. I do mean it. It's not his fault. He was only trying to help. He sits down at the table and motions for me to join him. So I do. I sit in the seat next to him and stare at the ground.

"It's not your fault…" I start. I hesitate to say what I want to say. "The guy I was with-"

He interrupts me, "Sadie, you really don't have to explain yourself. It's my fault I overstepped."

"I promise it's not your fault, Derek, it's not your fault you don't know," I say without looking up. We sit in silence for a minute. I stare at the ground.

I take a deep breath. "The first time he hit me, he said he was just mad and that he would never do it again," I confess to him.

"Sadie, you really don't have to," he says, but I stop him.

"I want you to know this. I trust you," I say. He nods, but I can tell he doesn't want me to continue. Like I'll break. He's not wrong.

"Then the next time it happened, he was drunk. I just thought he was a mad drunk. He was so sweet in the beginning, you know? It was hard to believe the boy I loved wanted to hurt me," I say, taking a long exhale. He lays his hand on the table open for me to grab. I set my hand in his as tears spill down my face. "It was frequent after that. He would call me names, then force me to do things I really didn't feel comfortable doing. If I didn't do what he said, he'd hit me." I finish slowly. My tears don't slow. He rubs his thumb against my hand and wipes the tears off my cheeks. I look up at him to see his eyes watering. We sit in silence. Like he's taking it all in. I can't believe I just told him all of that.

"I'm sorry I didn't mean to upset you," I say quietly. He looks into my eyes.

"You didn't upset me. I just—" He runs a hand down his face, shaking his head. "It kills me to hear that someone hurt you like that. That they got away with it. You deserve to feel safe and to feel loved, Sadie," he says as he looks at me. "I don't know how you're still standing after all of that, but I'm really glad you are. You are strong, Sadie, stronger than I've ever been," his voice catching in his throat.

I tilt my head slightly and look at him. "What do you mean by that?" I ask gently.

He hesitates. Glances down at his arms on the table. "You saw them, didn't you?" he mumbles, not looking at me. I don't answer right away. He finally looks up, and I nod slowly. He lets go of my hand and rolls up his sleeves, exposing his tender arms. "I um- I used to…" He stammers. "Back when everything fell apart. After my football career was shattered, after a million different meds, after I didn't recognize my own life anymore," he says, voice shaking. "It felt like the only thing I could control. Then, eventually, I couldn't control it anymore, and that's when my parents forced me to get help," he finishes.

I lift my hand and set it on his arm. "I haven't in a while, I'm better now," he says quietly. He sniffles, then gives a small smile.

I nod, because I understand. "Pain can do that. Blind us, makes us reach for anything that might make it stop. even if it causes more damage." I pause, sitting in the silence. "But you pulled yourself out. That matters. That says a lot about who you are." I squeeze his hand carefully. "And I'm really glad you're still here, Derek."

He lets out a shaky breath, eyes still on our hands. "Yeah. I am, too." He glances up at me, and a grateful smile tugs on his lips. Eyes still glossy, he says, "Wow, I never cry."

I giggle quietly. "Sooo, I think we need some ice cream," I say.

He rolls his eyes. "Fine, whatever you want." He responds by putting the paint away. It's 2 am. "Good thing Skippy's is 24/7," he continues. I laugh and pack up the rest of the stuff. I stretch my arms wide and give him a soft smile as he embraces me in a hug.

"You're a good friend, Derek," I say, not letting go right away. He doesn't say anything.

Eventually, he pulls away and grabs my face. "Let's get you that shake, shall we?" he says. I nod.

8

~while it lasts

We're exhausted the next day. Basically, falling asleep while painting our leaves. My hair is thrown into a messy claw clip to get it out of my face, and my hands are speckled with green paint.

"You're going way too dark," I say, looking at his leaves.

He glances at me, smiling. "No, I'm adding depth. It's called dimension."

I scoff and dip my brush into a lighter green just to spite him. "If you say so. You're lucky I'm too tired to argue that." I say, leaning against the wall and closing my eyes.

"Sadie, do not fall asleep on me," he says, rolling his eyes.

"It's your fault I'm so tired," I say without opening my eyes.

"Yeah, yeah, I guess," he says, dipping his paint in the green. We fall into an easy rhythm. For once, we're not overthinking it. Just doing what feels right for us.

Clara walks in and claps her hands once. It startles me awake. "Okay, guys, I'm going to group you up with another pair to give each other feedback," she says as a girl and a guy trail in behind her.

"Hi, I'm Levi," the guy says.

"And I'm Tess," the girl with the long black hair I saw on the first day says. Tess is pretty. Her long black hair falls almost to her hips. Her style reminds me of someone who would live in the mountains in Colorado. Levi is almost the same. His mullet under his baseball cap shows his brown, loose curls. He's wearing cowboy boots and jeans. He looks unbothered.

"Derek," Derek says, turning toward them.

"Sadie, nice to meet you guys," I say, smiling.

We stand there awkwardly waiting for Clara to leave, but she just looks around at us, smiling.

"Okay, well, I will let you guys get to it," she says as she turns to leave. We all kind of snicker, and they set their stuff down.

"This looks so good, I'm loving the dimension in the leaves," Tess says. My head drops, and I hear Derek chuckle.

I turn to whack his arm while laughing, "Shut up, Derek," I say, still laughing.

Tess looks at me and cocks her head, and smiles.

"I like it, I really don't have any feedback other than the top half is missing, but I have a feeling you already knew that," Levi says. We laugh. "Want to check out ours?" he asks. We nod and get up to walk down the skinny hallway to their room. They open their door to expose a half-drawn ocean on the bottom half and a bright sky on the top. It's beautiful. I've always had a secret love for the ocean.

"Wow, this is really good, guys," Derek says, walking in.

"Thanks," Tess says, looking it up and down.

"I think you guys should add something into the ocean, like something floating," I say, glancing at Levi.

"Oooo, I like that, thanks, Sadie," Levi says, nodding multiple times.

"Great, so we gave our feedback, wanna get some food?" Derek asks.

"Yes," we all say. We laugh and walk to Skippy's again. I swear we have gone every night this week. But it's within walking distance, so it'll have to do.

"Sooo are you and Levi dating?" I ask Tess. The boys follow a little bit behind us, looking at their phones.

"Nah," Tess says, looking down. "I have a boyfriend back home, and Levi's not really my type," she finishes, looking at me. Eyes squinting because of the sun.

"Ahh, gotcha," I say, opening the diner door, and everyone follows me close behind. I sit on one side of the booth, and Derek scooches in next to me. Tess and Levi are on the other side.

"Are you getting a latte?" Derek whispers in my ear.

"Yes, and some pancakes," I respond, turning to look at him and smiling. We order, and Levi and Derek get up to check out the jukebox in the corner.

Tess looks up from the table at me, "So are you and Derek dating?" she asks in a teasing tone.

"No, we are not, we're just friends," I say, smiling at her. I like her, she's very similar to me.

"Mk," she says, rolling her eyes but smiling. They come back to the table just as our food comes.

"I really like your guys' painting," Tess says, glancing at me. "How did you come up with the idea of just doing a simple tree?" she asks.

I look at Derek and laugh. "It was the first thing that came to mind," I say.

"But it was Sadie's idea to make it seem weathered and look tired," Derek says, nudging my arm. Tess smiles and scratches the top of her head.

"Oh, well, I just know it'll turn out great," Levi says.

"Yes, so will your ocean," I say through a mouthful of pancakes.

Derek looks at Levi and Tess across the booth, "So what brings you guys here?" he blurts.

"Derek," I mutter under my breath, glaring at him.

"Nah, it's cool, I've been wondering the same, not gonna lie," Levi says. "Straight up, I'm depressed, have been for my whole life, it feels like. Thought I would try something new," he says, shrugging his shoulders. "Like I'm good but I want to be better, ya know," he finishes.

I nod slowly, "Respect," I smile at him. He smiles and continues eating his hash browns.

Tess takes a deep breath. "My younger brother has a lot of medical issues," she says, looking up from her phone.

"Oh, I'm sorry, Tess," Derek replies.

"No, it's okay. I've been dealing with it my whole life, you know. Eventually, I got tired of being looked through, and I started acting out. Took my parents a while to even notice, but once they did, they didn't even hear me out, they just sent me here," she finishes, half smiling.

Levi puts his arm around her. Their friendship reminds me of a brother/sister dynamic. I wish my brother were protective of me like that.

"I blew out my knee last year," Derek says and shrugs, "no biggie," he finishes. I know it's a big deal. I know he might be better now, but part of me thinks he isn't past it yet.

"That sucks, I'm sorry," Tess says, looking at Derek. It's quiet. I haven't looked up in a minute. Oh, they're all staring at me.

"Sadie?" Tess says, looking in my direction. "You don't have to tell us if you don't want to," she finishes.

"No, um, it's cool, I just was in a bad situation I stayed in too long, that's all," I say, messing with the leftover pancake on my plate. It's silent for a while, but Tess reaches across to grab my hand.

"Hmm, nothing like trauma bonding in the middle of a diner on a Thursday evening," Levi says. We all laugh, and Tess jokingly pushes him. It's not much, but it feels like the start of something.

* * *

Tess gave me her number after we ate. It'll be nice to have another female friend here. Derek walked me back to my room and said he'd see me tomorrow. My phone buzzes as I shut the door behind me. It's Tess. I turn on my LED lights and throw on a random movie.

Tess: *hiii*
just wanted to say i'm really glad we hung out today
Me: *me too*
thanks for being... normal. and kind.
Tess: *you don't have to thank me for that*
we should make a group chat
Me: *yeah lets do it*

She makes a group chat with Levi and Derek, but they immediately start sending stupid memes that don't interest me. I put my phone down and go to change into pajamas. I grab some shorts and a hoodie from the back of my closet I haven't seen in a while. I stare at it for a while until I realize when the last time I wore it was.

We had just fought. He had said I was too sensitive but also too desperate. I had spent the whole walk home quiet, trying not to cry. He showed up at my house later that night when my parents were asleep.

He knocked, holding my least favorite candy and a fake smile. "I figured you'd be over it by now," he says, stepping in before I could have even answered. I wasn't over it.

He sat down on my bed and started rubbing my shoulders. Hard.

"I said some stupid stuff. You know I didn't mean it," he said. I felt tense and unsure if he meant that.

"I just hate when you make me feel like the bad guy," he adds, a little colder. He started kissing my neck, and I froze.

"Chase, I don't really feel like—" I say softly but firmly.

"Let's just not fight tonight, okay?" he said into my skin. "Just do it," he finished, pulling me back further onto the bed. My body had gone limp, and I couldn't even remember if he had even apologized.

I drop the hoodie on the floor like it's on fire. I press my fingers into my head, the fabric still clinging to the smell of that night. Cheap Chinese food and overbearing cologne. My chest tightens. I grab a different hoodie and shove the other one into the back of my closet on the floor. I pick up my phone and swipe out of meme central and into my texts with Tess.

Me: *are u busy rn?*

Tess: *no why*

Me: *want to go for a walk?*

Tess: *sure!*

I find her in the lobby. She's wearing the same thing as earlier, even though it's 7 pm. I'm in my sweat set.

"Hey girl," she says with a smile.

"Hi," I respond, reaching to open the door.

"Where are we gonna go?" she asks, stepping through the door behind me.

"I dunno, maybe just around by Main Street?" I glance at her.

"Sure sounds good," she says, putting her hands in her pockets. I trust her even though I hardly know her. That's rare for me now. I was a really trusting person before. Obviously a little too trusting.

"Are you good?" she asks, turning toward me.

"Yeah, I just needed some fresh air," I say quietly.

"Are you normally this guarded?" she asks out of nowhere.

I smile and turn in her direction. "Are you normally this blunt?" I say. We both laugh as we get close to Main Street.

"Honestly, yes, I am," she says, still laughing.

"Okay, good to know," I laugh and look down at my tennis shoes. I take a breath, "No, I wasn't always like this."

"What made you like this then?" she asks.

"More of a who," I start. "My ex…" I say, looking toward her.

"Oh, I'm sorry," she says, grabbing my hand for a moment. "Does Derek know?" she asks.

"Yeah, I told him all of it last night, actually," I say. She nods. "Okay, next topic," I say.

"Okay, fine, but we will be revisiting," she says, smiling. I nod and laugh. We walk down Main Street, lit up and alive with people. Small-town Connecticut isn't half bad. I thought it would be boring and empty, but it's far from it. I know there are a couple of colleges around here. Maybe if I like it enough here, I'll stay. But I'm far from making any life-altering decisions right now.

"Let's talk about Derek then and what's going on there," she says, nudging her elbow to my arm.

I roll my eyes, "We are just friends," I say, smiling.

"Not the way he looks at you, girl," she responds.

"Nah, he doesn't see me like that," I say, putting my head down.

"Mmk," she says, "maybe I should ask him."

"Um, absolutely not."

"I'm joking!" she exclaims. "C'mon, let's get a milkshake from the ice cream stand," she says, motioning in that direction. I nod and follow her, the smell of waffle cones getting stronger with each step.

Maybe tonight I can make everything feel different. Maybe it's enough to just walk, laugh, and drink something sweet under string lights with a new friend.

For the first time in a long time, I think it's time I let myself enjoy my life just a little bit more.

9

~glowing

I love the weekends. I always have. I think more than the average person. Weekends feel like summer. Like, I get a break. No obligations. Except now that I am here, weekends are boring. I used to spend them sledding with Julia during the winter or going to farmers' markets with my mom in the summer. Now I get to sit in my room and wait for the next day and the next day to come.

It's Friday night, and instead of going out to a bar or a club like a normal 21-year-old, I'm listening to a podcast on influencers and how they're ruining the internet. I feel like I'm wasting my favorite time of the year by sitting and painting, and then sitting some more.

I change into my pajamas when I get a knock on my door. Derek. I open the door to see him standing with a duffel bag.

"Hi, Sadie," he says as he pushes his way past me into my room.

"Hi, did we have plans tonight that I forgot about?"

"Nah, but now we do," he says. I cock my head and look at him, smiling. "Pack a bag, we're going to New York City," he says, all giddy.

"What do you mean we're going to New York City?" I respond by crossing my arms.

"I know you've always wanted to go, and it's only like a 2-hour drive," he continues, "so we're going. Besides, what else do we have to do this weekend?" he says. I can't help but smile. He remembered. "Chop chop, it's already 8:00," he finishes.

"Okay, okay!" I say as I jump up a couple of times and clap my hands together. He waits on my couch while I pack my bag and change into a New York City-worthy outfit. I can't wait until I can tell Julia this.

We throw our stuff in the back seat of his matte black Lexus. I didn't know he drove, and I hop into the front seat.

"So where are we even gonna stay?" I ask.

"Don't worry, I booked us a hotel right near Times Square," he says as he buckles his seat belt.

"Isn't that expensive?" I ask.

"Mm, don't worry about that," he says as he shifts it into gear. I roll my eyes and take off my shoes to sit cross-legged on his seat.

"Okay, fine, but can we please get McDonald's first?" I ask by giving him puppy dog eyes.

"Of course we can," he says, turning his wheel to the nearest McDonald's. He pulls up to the window and looks at me to tell him what I want.

"I want a chicken nugget happy meal," I say with a smile. He rolls his eyes and proceeds to order it. We don't talk much on the way there, instead, he cranks the music and rolls the windows down as we drive on the highway. It makes me feel rejuvenated. Something I haven't felt in a long time. He's a good friend for doing this for me, even though he said it was stinky and crowded there.

We finally pull into the valet service. Never thought I'd say that sentence. It's close to 11:00 since there was traffic. I hardly noticed it.

We step into the lobby, warm with gold light and quiet music, fancier than I expected. Derek moves like he's been here before. I fall behind taking it all in.

"Yep, reservation under Derek Callahan... yes, two rooms," he says to the receptionist. The lady nods, types something in, and hands him two cards. Derek turns and hands me a card.

"You're in 1032. I'm next door." That's all he says with a smile.

I grab the card from him and grip my bag. "Thank you," I say, looking at him. "Seriously."

He shrugs and smiles softly. "No biggie. Besides, I snore," he says, motioning me toward the elevator. The elevator ride is quiet. Very few people in my life have done things like this for me. He's not only a good friend, he's the first person in a long time who's let me exist without needing anything in return.

"Okay, drop your bag in your room, we're going down to Times Square," he says, opening his door next to mine. His smile might be brighter than all of Times Square. I do what he says, and we head back down. He grabs my hand and practically drags me out to the street.

"This is even more amazing than I've ever imagined," I say, twirling around looking at all the lights. "This is all I've ever dreamed of," I smile at him. He doesn't say anything. He just watches me spinning in circles so I don't miss anything on the billboards.

When I stumble a little from spinning too fast, he steadies

me with both hands gently and lets me go.

"I like seeing you like this," he says finally.

"Like what?" I ask, catching my breath from spinning.

He shrugs, looking away for a second. "Like... you don't feel so heavy. I feel like I'm seeing the real Sadie," he says with a soft smile.

I don't know what to say to that. But he's right. I feel a little lighter today. But I look at him a little longer, and he holds my gaze, just for a second. Then he clears his throat. "C'mon," he says, "let's check out the rest," as he begins to walk the other direction, and I follow.

We walk around for a while, checking out the different vendors. It's almost 1:00 in the morning now, and my phone buzzes in my pocket. Julia is calling me, and I am just wondering how in the world I'm supposed to explain this. I answer the FaceTime anyway.

"Hi, Sad- wait, where are you?" she asks, shoving her face closer to the phone.

I cover my mouth and laugh before answering, "Umm Times Square ...?" I say as I pan the camera to Derek. He holds up a peace sign and looks back at me as I laugh again.

"Sadie, that's like your dream," she says with a huge smile.

"I know, I know," I say as I turn the camera so Derek can't see anymore. "Derek planned this, and we just got here a couple of hours ago," I finish.

"He brought you there? Sadie..." she says, giving me that look she always does.

I nod, "We're having fun."

"You're glowing, Sades," she says with a soft smile. "I've missed this version of you," she says.

"Me too," I admit. "I wish you were here too, though."

She smiles, "Me too, but I hope you have the best time with Derek," she says, and raises her eyebrows a couple of times. I roll my eyes at her.

"I love you, I'll send pics."

She nods, "Love you too, girl, be safe," she responds. I nod and hang up the FaceTime. I don't put my phone away, but instead take out the camera.

"Derek, smile for a selfie," I say, putting my phone in the air. He gets close and smiles for the camera. I send the picture to our group chat with Tess and Levi before putting my phone away. I twirl around once more, taking in everything.

Derek's watching me again. It kind of makes me nervous.

"You good?" he asks with a lopsided smile.

"Yeah," I breathe out. "Better than good."

We start walking back toward the hotel. The streets are still busy, but quieter now. This city never sleeps. How could it?

"You didn't have to do all this," I say, looking over at him as we walk.

He shrugs, not looking at me. "I wanted to."

I smile as we reach the lobby and wait for the elevator in silence. On our floor, we step out and stop by our doors. "Alright," I say, "Goodnight, Derek. Thank you. Seriously." I say as I buzz open my door.

He nods. Smiles a little. "Of course."

"See you in the morning bright and early, right?" I ask him.

He gives a small nod, "Goodnight, Sadie," and slips into his own room.

I close my door lightly behind me and look around the room in awe. The view from my window overlooks Times Square, which I can tell is near where the ball drops on New Year's Eve. When I would watch the ball drop growing up, I would imagine being here. In this place, with all the lights, and bundled up to protect myself from the cold. I could have made the trip if I really wanted to. But no one ever wanted to come with me.

I double-check the door is locked before climbing into my queen-size bed that I have all to myself. Selecting the best pictures to send to Julia is quite the task. There were already too many to even choose from. But I do, before turning off my phone and entering my favorite part of the day.

Sleep.

10

~is there more?

Derek: *you up?*

It's 8:00 in the morning. I already have my jeans on and a tight purple long-sleeve top that shows just a little of my stomach. My teeth are brushed, and my hair is done.

Me: *Yes*

Derek: *can you be ready in 20?*

I like his message and start on some light makeup and pack my purse. I have a list of things I would love to see in New York, but I wonder if he has anything planned. He knocks on my door, and I open it with a smile.

"Ready?" he says with a smile. He has on blue jeans and a brown crew neck. I nod and shut the door behind me. "Okay, I have a few things for us to do, but first is coffee, obviously," he says, stepping into the elevator.

"Music to my ears," I say, and place my purse on my shoulder. The coffee shop is just down the street. It's so cute, of course.

"An iced vanilla latte with almond milk, please," I say to the barista. "Oh, and a bagel," I add.

"Make that two bagels," he says, coming up behind me.

"$30.73," the barista says. Derek pushes my hand out of the way and pulls out his wallet. I roll my eyes, but I let him pay anyway.

"Thank you," I say as I go to the other end of the counter. He nods and motions me toward a table in the corner.

"So, I'm not confident in how to use the subway, but we'll figure it out," he says, taking a bite of his bagel.

"It can't be that hard," I say and giggle. "This is so good. I've always wanted to try a New York coffee," I add, taking a sip.

"I'm glad you like it. We're going to that Statue of Liberty first, then to Central Park," he says, looking at me.

"That sounds perfect." I take out my phone and snap a picture of our bagels and coffee, Derek caught mid-look to the side, and post it to my Instagram story.

"Alright, let's go figure out the subway," he says as he gets up from the table.

We figure it out, no problem. We laugh watching people who look very confused or are running to catch their train. It's busy, but Derek let me have the last seat, and he stood in front of me.

The ferry ride over to the Statue of Liberty is cold, but beautiful. I look off to the side of the boat while the skyline shrinks behind us and the statue comes into view. Derek sits next to me the whole time, pointing out things he remembers from a middle school field trip. When we finally got up close, I'm surprised by how big it actually is. We walk around the base, take a few photos, and sit on a bench people watching for a while. Just enjoying the view. Enjoying the time I get to spend here unexpectedly.

Next stop is Central Park. It is huge. Bigger than any photo

I've seen. We wander around for a while with no real plan. No place to go. I love Central Park. It's interesting to me how it's like the calm in the middle of a big city. It's just a park.

I tuck a strand of hair behind my right ear and look at him. He's watching some birds swarm a lady with food. "This is really nice," I say, looking up at him.

"Yeah?" he asks, his eyes warm.

I nod as his hand brushes against mine, and for a split second, I thought about grabbing his hand. But why would I do that? I know he doesn't see me like that. If he did, he would've made a move by now. Maybe it's for the best right now, though. He's reliable.

"I'm glad I got to be the one to take you here," he says, almost whispering it.

I don't say anything and just keep walking ahead toward the street performer.

"You know, I've always wanted to try a street hot dog," I say, pointing to the little cart down the street.

He smiles and looks toward the hot dog stand. "Well then, we have to get one," he says, grabbing my arm and pulling me toward it.

I take a huge bite. "This is so good!" I say with a mouth full of a hot dog covered in all the toppings. He laughs at me and grabs it out of my hand to take a bite too. He nods approvingly.

"So, when are we heading back?" I ask him while sitting on a park bench.

He sits next to me. "Probably late tomorrow morning," he crosses his left leg over his right. "I got us two nights in the hotel," he says as he leans back on the bench.

"Okay, yay! What are we going to do tonight?" I ask him.

"What do you want to do?"

"I want to try some New York pizza," I say, looking over at him.

He nods and takes another bite of the hot dog. "I can make that happen," he says, smiling at me.

"And maybe we can find somewhere where we can see all the city lights?"

"Okay, I can maybe make that happen," he says, finishing the hot dog. I smile and look around at all the people. To think they're all just strangers. Just like Derek and I were not to long ago.

We find a pizza place near our hotel. It's delicious just as I had imagined it would be. I got pepperoni, and Derek got sausage. He eats like no one is watching. Sauce smeared all over his face.

I laugh at him before telling him. Even though I'm sure he already knows. "You got a little something," I say, motioning my hand over my face. He rolls his eyes and laughs like he doesn't really care if anyone sees him like that.

He finally wipes his face. "I found out we can get up to the rooftop of the hotel, so we should go up there to see the city lights," he says, putting his napkin on top of his plate.

I smile and clap my hands, "yay, I'm excited!"

It's starting to get dark out, so we head back and grab a drink from the hotel bar. We sit at the bar for a while. We don't really talk, just exchange glances every once in a while.

I'm almost finished with my drink when Derek nudges my arm, "You ready?" I nod and chug the rest of my drink before following him to the elevator. My social battery is running low, but it doesn't matter when you're in New York City. I could do this all night if I'm here. We head up 75 floors before reaching the top.

He opens the rooftop door, and a cold breeze hits my face. I can't see far, but it's bright. The echo of cars buzzing in the background. "Wow," I whisper and follow him to the railing. I can't help but smile. It's so bright and full of life. I wonder if I would have ever been able to see this if my parents hadn't sent me to New Haven.

"I feel like I'm on top of the world. Like I'm bigger than the city," I finally say.

"Yeah," he replies. "But somehow it makes us look small?"

I look around at all the lights. Shining onto his face. It's making him glow gold.

"You know, I think I forgot what it feels like to be around someone who doesn't make me feel small," I say as I turn toward him and lean my arm on the railing.

He takes a breath and turns his head in my direction without looking away from the city. "You should never be afraid to take up space in this world," he says, moving his eyes to meet mine.

I look away from him. I breathe deeply. "I don't really do things like this," I admit.

"What, go to the rooftop of a fancy hotel?" he teases.

I laugh. "No. Let people in."

He looks at me. Really looks at me. "Thank you for letting me."

I smile and close my eyes for a moment and feel the breeze on my body. I let out a shiver, and I feel Derek drape his jacket onto my shoulders. "Thank you," I say. He just nods and looks back out as I do. It's late. But this city never sleeps.

I feel safe with Derek. His friendship feels like a warm summer day. For once, I feel seen, needed. It's been a long time since I've felt secure in that way. I've only known him for a a little while, but it feels like we've been friends forever. I think in one way or another, he just gets me. He understands me. I wouldn't want anything to ruin what we have as friends.

But what if there's something more?

11

~out of tune

"Hiiii Sadieee," Tess says when I walk into Derek's apartment. She's sitting on the couch with her legs criss-crossed and a drink in front of her. "I already made you a drink," she says, smiling, handing me a red drink in one of Derek's glasses.

We came back from New York yesterday. The drive during the day is kind of boring, but Derek let me read my book while he drove. The trip was amazing. I think I could have explored for at least another week if I had the time. Maybe one day I will.

I grab the cup from her hands. "Thank you," I say and smile at her as I sit next to her on the couch. "Where are the boys?" I ask, taking a sip. It's delicious.

"They ran to the gas station to grab some snacks," she says, checking her watch. "They'll be back soon," she continues. I nod and look around Derek's apartment. "What were you doing before you came?" she asks.

"I just had some cleaning to do and stuff," I say, looking back at her.

She nods. "Sooo tell me about New York!"

"It was absolutely incredible," I say, "better than I have ever imagined."

"So did y'all kiss?" she says, raising her eyebrows mockingly.

"Um, oh my gosh?" I say, hitting her arm, "No, we did not, it's not like that." I say, laughing at her.

"Yeah, because my guy friend just randomly plans trips to the big apple, but no, that doesn't mean a thing," she says, doing air quotes when she said guy friend. I roll my eyes.

I am about to tell her about everything we did when Derek and Levi come back, so I stop myself.

"Oh, hi, Sadie, glad you made it," Derek says, smiling. Levi plops down on the rug in front of me and stares at his phone. He moves his hair out of his face and lies down with his elbows behind him, holding himself up. He stretches his legs out and doesn't look up from his phone. He always seems so relaxed. Like everything he does is effortless.

"Hi Derek," I say, locking eyes with him. He sets his snacks down and sits next to me on the couch, and leans in close to me.

"What are you drinking?" he asks, peering into my glass.

"I dunno Tess made it," I responded by handing it to him. "Try it," I say.

"Yes, ma'am," he says and takes a swig from the glass. He nods and hands it back to me. "Not bad." I smile and take the glass back. "I like your new shoes," he whispers in my ear.

I smile but don't reply. I had ordered them before we went to New York, and they came in yesterday. My mom let me use her card as my reward for making it here this long.

"Hi Levi," I say softly, looking back at him.

He slaps his phone down dramatically, "What's up, Harper?"

he says with a smile. I stare at him for a second too long. Like I was zoned out looking at him. I can't even lie, Levi is attractive. He's tall, probably 6'3". His arm muscles show through his t-shirt. I smile at him before looking away. But I can tell, he's still looking at me.

"So there's karaoke at the bar down the street," Tess says, looking up from her phone. "Do you guys want to go?" she asks. I don't really want to, but I remembered what my parents say about branching out and saying yes. Maybe I will have fun. I really like the little friend group I've made here so far.

"I'm down," Derek says. "C'mon, Sadie, I know you wanna read or something, but this will be fun," he says, looking at me and giving me extreme puppy dog eyes.

I nod slowly, "Okay, fine," I relent.

"Yay!" Tess says and claps her hands. "Okay, let's go," she says, getting up. I drop my head back dramatically, and Derek grabs my arm and drags me off the couch.

* * *

The bar is very full. It's a mix between people our age and older women singing songs from the '80s. Something my mom would do for sure. I'm 21 now, so it's nice that I can participate in these things even if my brain says I shouldn't. We sit down at a table near the middle but off to the side so we can all see the little stage. Tess starts showing me pictures of her and her boyfriend. He has short blonde hair and looks almost like a celebrity that I can't seem to place. I nod and say "oh, cute" every once in a while. Derek and Levi are laughing at some video game memes I don't understand, even though they showed it to me and tried to explain.

"I'll take a vodka cran," I say when the waitress comes around. She's tatted and has several piercings. She nods and looks toward Derek.

"Beer, whatever you have on tap is fine," he says.

"Me too," Levi chimes in, looking up from his phone.

"I'll just have a seltzer," Tess says. The waitress nods and is back with them in a few minutes. I sit quietly in the corner. Watching Derek quietly. He's been through things I would have never imagined. He seems happy and content with where he's at. Maybe I'm just not as good at hiding how I feel. But then again, I had to hide everything for a long time. It has become exhausting. Like no one gets to see the real you, and I guess that's almost the point of being here. My mom said it should help me get out of my shell.

I was never introverted. Always loud, always talking to everyone at the party, and making new friends. Now that seems impossible to do. But I think eventually I'll get there. If anyone seems like the type to pull me out of my shell, it would be my new little friend group.

"Sadie, can you sing?" Tess asks.

I shrug, "not really," I say.

"She's lying." Derek sips his drink and purposely avoids eye contact. "She can sing."

I glare at him as he snickers. Of course, he would do that.

"You have to do a song," Tess says, grabbing my shoulders.

"Whyyyyy," I whine and give Derek a fake stink eye.

"C'mon, Sadie, do it," Levi says, nudging me off my chair.

I roll my eyes and start to get up out of my chair. "Fine."

The mic squeals a little as I step onto the small stage, the lights are a little too bright, and the room is suddenly too quiet. I glance back at them. Levi gives me a thumbs-up, and my stomach does a flip. I adjust the mic down to my height. I scroll through the song list and find it. *The Night We Met*. Nostalgic. My finger hovers for a second, then taps the song.

The first few notes flow through the speakers, and the background chatter fades to nothing. I look down at my feet perched on the little stool on stage. I wrap my fingers around the mic.

My voice wavers a little at first, but then it finds itself. Like it never really left. I don't look at anyone. The words of the song pull memories out of me I didn't know I was still carrying. My eyes lock with Derek, and he doesn't move them off of me. But I look away from him.

The next lyrics flow out of me and into the microphone. Like they've been dying to escape. Dying to be let out. Dying to be heard. My watering eyes make the lights blur. My throat tightens. I keep going anyway. I finish the majority of the song before I want to get off stage. The stage is not where I belong. But I've loved this song since high school.

When I finish, there's a quick period of silence before most people in the room clap. I killed the mood. I should've picked a lighter song. I finally look up and out to the audience. Tess's jaw is on the floor. And Derek... he's looking at me like he's never really seen me before. Like he just witnessed a new part of me.

I half-smile at the audience and rush off the stage back to my seat.

"You were incredible," Tess says, smiling at me. The bar has already moved on to the next drunk girl singing Katy Perry.

"You sounded great, Sades," Derek says, looking at me and cocking his head to the left.

Tess leans in to whisper something over the noise. "Come

to the bathroom with me quickly."

I nod and get up and follow her to the back of the bar. The bathroom is dark but lit by some yellow lights above the mirrors.

"What's up?" I ask her. She looks uncomfortable. "Is everything okay?" I press.

"I um- overheard Derek and Levi talking right before you started," she says, twirling her hair.

"Okay..?"

She hesitates, "Levi said something about the NYC trip to Derek and asked if something is going on between you two," she starts. I nod slowly while still listening. "He said it wasn't like that and that it wasn't some grand gesture or whatever. He just figured you needed to get away," she finishes.

My chest tightens. "Well, I guess he's not wrong, I mean, we aren't a thing, so he can feel however he wants." My voice catches in my throat, and I quickly tuck my hair behind my ears.

"Okay, but then," she pauses, "he, uh, said that it didn't mean anything," Tess says, grabbing my hand. Those words hit harder than expected. "I'm sorry, I just wanted you to know," she says, pulling me in for a hug. My arms remain at my sides. I stare at the wall behind her.

"It's fine, it's not a big deal, I know he doesn't see me like that," I say. "And I don't see him like that. We're friends," I finish.

"Are you okay?" she asks, pulling away.

"Yes, I'm fine, I promise," I say as we walk out of the bathroom. "I'm gonna grab another drink," I say and head toward the bar. She nods and goes back to the table. I order a drink and four shots for us and bring them back to our table.

"Ohhh shots," Levi says, grabbing one off the tray.

"Mhm, " I say, handing the rest out. We do them together, and the waitress comes back, and I ask for another round.

"Are you good?" Derek asks, eyes on me.

I nod and smile wide and bright.

I don't mean it.

12

~spacing

I avoid Derek for a few days. I tell him I'm sick and need a few days off from painting. I can't really be mad about what he said, can I? Sometimes the truth hurts. I just need a break from everyone. But I do need some interaction. I grab my phone and hit Julia's name. No answer. Voicemail it is.

"Hi Jules, um, just call me back when you get this. I need someone to talk to," I say into my phone. I slam it onto the couch, but it buzzes. I pick it up and hope it's Julia calling me back. It's not. It's a therapy reminder. I grab my laptop and plop on my couch. Honestly, I need advice, so this could be beneficial.

"So, Derek is my mural partner, and he took me to New York City last weekend and took care of everything," I say to my computer screen.

"Well, that was nice of him," my therapist, Jill, says.

"So I thought maybe he liked me because that's kind of a big gesture, you know, but my other friend Tess, that I met here, said that she overheard him tell our other friend Levi that it didn't mean anything." I continue.

"Well, how did that make you feel?" she asks, like I knew she would.

"Honestly, terrible, even though we never talked about feelings or anything, it kind of hurt, you know." I spit out. "I thought there was some sort of connection, but I guess I was wrong."

She gives me a soft smile. "Even so, I don't think it's a smart idea for you to jump into a new relationship right away while you're still healing from the last, Sadie," she says sincerely. Like she actually cares.

I nod. "You're right, I'll just pretend like I don't know what he said and just be his friend. Because he is a good friend," I say.

She nods and writes something down on her notepad on her desk. "What about this Tess?" she asks.

"Oh, I like her, we have a lot in common," I say with a half smile.

"That's good. I'd work on furthering that friendship and focus on your healing and your painting," she says, "I believe in you, you're doing great," she finishes.

"Okay, I can do that, thanks, Jill," I say.

"You're welcome, we'll pick up in a few weeks," she replies.

"Sounds good, bye," I say and end the call. I close my laptop and take a deep breath. I should go today. I can't let him fend for himself for much longer.

My corner spot is open, so I plop down with another latte and scroll on my phone. Legs propped on the little table when I hear footsteps. I don't look up as I figure it's going to be Derek.

"Harperrrr," a familiar voice says.

I finally look up, "Oh, hi Levi." I'm surprised to see him.

71

"Haven't seen you in a couple of days," he says, sitting in the chair next to me.

"Yeah, sorry… I was sick?" I say, raising my voice and octave at the end of my sentence.

"Righttt," he says, looking at me. He takes a deep breath. "Um, what are you doing tonight?" he asks.

"Probably nothing, why?" I say putting my phone away.

"Do you want to do something?" he asks slowly.

I hesitate before I say anything. "With Tess and Derek, too?"

He glances down, "uh, no… just us?" he says slowly.

"Oh," I pause, "sure that would be fun." I give him a soft smile as I start to get up. "I gotta go, Derek is probably waiting for me, I'll text you later, okay?"

"Yeah, sounds good," he says with a smile. I nod and walk to our room.

I have to tell Julia.

"Hi Derek," I say as I walk into our room. He's setting up the paints and is wearing his usual long sleeves and jeans. You can really see his muscles through his shirt.

"Hi, Sades, I've missed ya," he says, coming over to hug me. I let him hug me, but pull away quickly. I've missed him, too, but I can't forget what he said. "Are you feeling better?" he asks as he walks back to our tree.

"Yeah, thanks," I say, setting my stuff down. "Want to just get started?" I suggest, shrugging my shoulders slightly.

"Yeah, sure, let's do more of the leaves," he says, grabbing the green paint and his brush. I nod and do the same. We don't say much, just focusing on our leaves.

"So uh," he starts and takes a breath, "want to hang out tonight? We could get milkshakes or something," he says, turning toward me. Maybe I should lie and tell him I'm hanging out with Tess or something.

"I can't tonight," I hesitate before continuing, "Levi… asked me to hang out." I turn away from him.

"Oh," he says, looking a little disappointed, "that's fun," he says. It sounds more like a question, though.

"Yeah, sorry."

"No worries, I should probably clean up my apartment anyway," he turns back to our tree. I nod. Why do I feel guilty? I feel like he's mad I'm hanging out with Levi. But he doesn't have a right to be. If he's not interested and doesn't see me like that, then he doesn't get to be upset when I spend time with someone else. I hate how I feel sometimes when I'm with him. But other times, I don't know if I feel anything. Is he actually disappointed? Or do I think that because I want him to be? Do I want him to be jealous? We never said we liked each other. We're friends, that's all.

13

~closer

I slip my credit card out of my wallet when the cashier is done scanning my new books. Four, to be exact. BOGO's are very important to readers. I plan on finishing at least one of these by the end of the night. I don't foresee myself being with Levi all night. Everyone needs some alone time to end their day.

I exit the store and carefully set my bag into the basket of my bike. The wind brushes my hair across my face when I get close to my apartment. I waste no time cracking open my new book when I get back.

Sometimes it feels wrong to genuinely judge a book by its cover when picking out what to read. But I think it's the most important part, to catch a reader's eye when scanning through shelves of books. At least that's what I do.

After eight chapters, I remember I'm supposed to have plans tonight.

Me: *so what are we doing tonight*

I send the text and open my book right back up. I don't get

back into the book again before my phone buzzes.

Levi: *last week i found this cool spot to see the stars*

Me: *ohhh*

Levi: *yeah it was cool*

Me: *i bet*

Levi: *its supposed to be clear tn, u wanna go?*

Me: *yea sounds fun*

Levi: *bet meet me in the parking lot in 20*

I like his message and check the weather. It's only 55 degrees outside. My preferred temperature this time of year. I bookmark my page and change into jeans, a cute top, and my leather jacket that I thrifted in high school. I sit on my couch watching the time tick down. I want to be a little bit late, so I don't seem desperate.

The sun's almost gone by the time I meet him outside. The sky's fading into that soft kind of blue that feels warm and like everything can be calm. Even when it's not. He was right. Not a cloud in sight.

Levi's leaning against his gray pickup, hands in his pockets, looking off into the distance. It looks like he's been waiting, but not impatiently. He's wearing jeans, his normal cowboy boots, and a Carhartt hoodie. It's red. He sees me and smiles big.

"Hey," I say as I walk up.

He smiles. "Hey. You ready?"

I nod and smile. "Where is this place?" I ask as I get close to him.

"Um, like five minutes away," he says, walking to the other side of his pickup to open the door.

"Thank you," I say softly, getting in. He nods and closes the door behind me.

Even though I don't really know what to expect out of this, I just know I need to get out of my own head for a while.

"I brought a blanket and pillows we can set up in the bed of the truck and some snacks for ya," he says, looking over me as he drives.

I smile, "Perfect." We aren't in the middle of nowhere. Kind of in a secluded area, but there are other trucks here doing the same as us. That makes me feel a little bit better knowing I'm not alone. Even though I was scared of something happening, I know I need to stop thinking of the worst-case scenario. Not everyone is Chase. Not everyone wants to hurt me. I know that. I really do. Levi is gentle and quiet. I've watched him paint, and honestly, I don't think he could hurt a fly. He's careful, delicate, almost.

We pull in next to other trucks, but far enough away that they aren't invading our personal space. He hops out and grabs the things from the back. I watch as he lays down the blanket and pillows. He holds his hand out for me to grab to climb into the bed. I gladly take it. I lie back and look up at all the stars as he climbs in next to me.

"Here," he says, handing me a bag of popcorn.

"I love popcorn," I say, opening the bag.

"I know, Derek told me," he says, getting situated. My heart skips a beat. I freeze. Just for a moment.

"Derek told you that?" I ask, looking at him.

"Yeah, he said it a while ago," he says, shrugging. He remembers? He pulls out a speaker and plays some soft music. Loud enough for us but not for others around us to hear.

"Oh well, thank you," I say, munching on the popcorn. I lie almost flat on my back, looking at the sky. I spot the Big Dipper and point it out to him. He laughs when I say I prefer the little dipper. I take a deep breath and finally turn to look at him lying on his back. Before I can look away, he catches me looking at him.

"Hi, Sadie."

"Hi Levi," I reply without breaking eye contact.

He shifts to lie more on his side, propped up on one elbow. "So... be honest. Did you think this was gonna be lame?"

I smile, "Honestly? A little. But I was mostly worried about being cold." I say.

"Well, maybe you shouldn't rely on this thin leather jacket," he says, laughing.

I tug on the sleeves. "17-year-old Sadie wore this even when it was below freezing."

He nods, "Very intimidating."

I sit up on my elbow to face him like he did. "That's the vibe I was going for. Don't mess with me, I have trauma and good taste in music.'"

"A powerful combo," he says, laughing and fidgeting with the blanket. We stay quiet, but there's a hum of the other people talking around us.

"You, doing okay lately? I feel like I haven't really seen you since karaoke night. And don't say you were sick," he points his finger at me.

I roll my eyes and hesitate before answering. "Yeah. I've just been... thinking about a lot of stuff. Sometimes I overthink everything I'm doing and start to feel like I'm not even real. Have you ever done that?"

He laughs gently, "I know that feeling all too well," he says as he looks up at the sky.

I hesitate before asking him what I want to ask. "Has Derek said anything about New York?"

Levi turns back to me. He hesitates. "Not really, why?"

"Just wondering what people say when I'm not around," I say.

"I don't think anyone talks about you the way you think they do."

I shrug. "No?" I cock my head to the right.

"I think you're just trying really hard to keep your walls up with us, Sadie," he says. "But you don't have to, we don't judge you for anything," he finishes. "You know that, right?"

I nod and wait a while before responding. "I know you're right, I just don't want to admit it," I say, pushing him delicately and laughing.

"We're all here for a similar reason," he says.

"I know, I just have a hard time trusting new people," I say.

"I get it," he says, lying back down on his back. He doesn't say much else, and neither do I. I just lie there and count the stars. Too many to really count.

My mom used to say she'd try to count the freckles on my face, but she'd lose her place because I have so many. She'd even try to connect the dots with them, but it just looked like a blob. I miss my mom. I miss her every day, but I know that this independence is helping me overcome what I've been through. I don't even realize it, but I feel a thick tear fall off to the side of my face. I hear him turn toward me again.

"Sadie, what's wrong?" he asks, wiping the tear off my cheek.

"I'm sorry," I whisper. "I just... I don't know what I'm doing anymore. With any of this, with being here, with people." I pause, "Some days I feel like I'm this version of myself I don't even recognize anymore."

"I get it," he says quietly. "I really do," he pauses, still looking at me while I look at the sky. "You know, Sadie, I think sometimes we outgrow the version of ourselves that got us through the bad parts, and maybe part of us doesn't know who we're supposed to be after that," he finishes.

I close my eyes and breathe slowly through the tight feeling in my chest. "What if I never figure it out?" I ask quietly. He's quiet before he answers.

He takes a breath, "Then we take it out one day at a time," he says. "Like this. Just being here. Finding some sort of joy in the small things. Just... not giving up on ourselves or each other."

I turn to look at him. He's not smiling. He's just looking at me like I'm a real person. Not a problem, not broken, not a burden. And for the first time in a while, I let myself believe that I'm not those things. Even if I'm still figuring it out.

"Thank you, Levi," I say, cracking a smile. His arm moves toward mine.

"Always," he says, fingers wrapping around my hand. My heart skips a beat as he squeezes my hand and leaves his hand there for a moment.

I take a deep breath before saying what I need to say. I say all these things without giving hardly any context to anything. If they're my friends, they should understand. After all, he just told me he doesn't judge me. I can't be ashamed of what I went through.

I take a deep breath and look him dead in the eyes. "I was abused," I pause, and his jaw falls just a little. I shrug, "By my ex, for over a year," I say sharply. It's been dying to come out.

He exhales slowly. "Dang, Sadie," he says. For once, I'm glad he's not just saying he's sorry like everyone else does when they find out.

I spit out an unexpected laugh, "Yep, and I have a restraining order on him because he tried to kill me," I say, but immediately feel regret and that I am oversharing.

"Sorry…" I laugh hysterically and cover my mouth. "It's not funny," but I don't stop laughing.

"No, no, it's fine, I'm glad he's your ex." He pauses, glancing at me. "Because if he wasn't, this would be the worst pep talk in the world right now." I let out another laugh. He smiles, just a little.

"I can agree with that," I say.

"But for real," he says warmly, "I hate that you went through that. You didn't deserve it," he says, moving his hand up my arm.

My heart skips a beat. "Thanks, Levi." He moves in closer, but I get nervous and slowly move away. "Um, do you want to head back? It's getting pretty late," I say. He nods and sits up to start putting things away. He doesn't question it.

* * *

It's kind of weird that we all live in the same building. All of our apartments look the same yet are so different. He walks me to my apartment door and leans against the door frame as I unlock it. "I had fun tonight, thanks for taking me."

"Anytime. See you tomorrow, Harper," he winks and starts to back away. I feel like he wants to kiss me goodnight. But I don't know if I want that. Not yet. We lock eyes for a while before I finally go into my room.

"Goodnight."

"Goodnight," he says, walking away.

I shut the door, lean with my back against it, and slide all the way down to the floor. I sit there for a minute thinking about the whole night. I think he would've kissed me back if I tried. He's attractive and he's sweet and he's kind, but what is it that I am really looking for? I seriously don't know.

I guess I just need some time to figure that out.

14

~I need you

"Hey, how was your night with Levi?" Derek says as I walk into the room.

"It was good," I say, setting my stuff down. "How was your night?" I ask.

"Not too bad, just cleaned up and stuff," he says.

I nod. "I like how our tree is coming along," I grab my paint tray.

"Me too," he says.

Looking at our tree, we've actually gotten a lot done. The trunk is done, but I'm still working on the large roots. Some above the ground but most below. The large array of leaves is coming along just like we want it. We paint and paint. I work on the roots below the ground. They're more complicated than I originally thought they'd be. We've been working for a couple of hours. It's silent between us. Usually, we have music or meaningless conversations to fill the silence, but today, I guess he wanted the silence.

"Did I do something?" he blurts out.

I snap my head around to face him, "What?"

"I feel like you've been avoiding me or something," he says, putting his brush down.

"No, I'm not, I've just been uh tired," I say.

"Okay?"

I hesitate and look around the room, avoiding his eyes. "I'm sorry," I say quietly. He looks like he's got more to say.

He scoots closer to me. We go back to painting for a minute. The silence between us isn't awkward, but it's heavy. Full of everything we're not saying.

"Do you regret New York?" he asks. I immediately stop what I am painting.

"Why would I?" I reply sharply.

He shrugs, his voice low. "I don't know. I just… ever since, something's been different with you."

I set the brush down, and his eyes meet mine. "I loved New York, but you know it didn't mean anything, right?" I say, shrugging. He freezes, but his eyes don't move off of mine. I wasn't planning to say that. It slips out before I can catch it.

"I—" he starts, but nothing comes out after that.

I quickly stand up, and the stool scrapes the floor. "I think I'm going to head out, I'm sorry," I say

"Sadie, wait," he says, getting up off his stool. His hand moves slightly toward mine, but then he puts it down. I pack up my stuff and throw my bag over my shoulder before moving toward the door. "Sadie, please—"

But I'm already halfway out the door.

* * *

I breathe deeply as I lie on my couch. My bright LED lights shine onto my legs, and I flip on Spotify on my TV. I feel bad about how I left Derek. But I needed to get away. Maybe I shouldn't have said that to him. Maybe he doesn't realize what I meant by that, or that I know what he said to Levi. Things are getting too complicated with Derek. It's like I'm fighting with these emotions toward him, but I can't win no matter what I feel.

Today sucked, but at least I have music. Music is like a getaway from my head. Like, I can remove my brain for a while so it can stop thinking. Somehow, all the artists can just explain how I feel and make me feel better.

I open my computer to start writing when Feeling Whitney comes on the TV. I stare at the screen in disbelief that it's still on my playlist.

"Hey, babe, how was your day?" he asked loudly while gripping my thigh.

"Yeah, it was good," I responded. I carefully scooch away from him and toward the end of the couch. I could hear his heavy breathing as he kept moving his hand up and up.

"Oh, babe, it's our favorite song," he continues, his hand up my thigh and under my skirt. "Feeling Whitney is his best work," he kept talking.

"Actually, I don't think I'm in the mood, Chase," I say as I pull my leg away from him.

"The hell you aren't," he said as he spread my legs apart and pushed me hard into the end of the couch. My eyes dart in every direction as I scramble away from his grasp. He just holds on tighter.

The present crashes back like a wave. I grab around the couch for my remote to skip the song. My breathing becomes heavy, and I reach for my phone off the charger.

Me: *I need you*
Derek: *I know*

I raise my eyebrow as I hear a faint knock on my door. I slowly open the door and see Derek standing there with takeout.

"I'm sorry about earlier, but I thought you could use some company."

I smile, but begin to cry at the same time.

"What's going on, Sadie? You can talk to me," he says as he places his hand on my shoulder and guides me back into my room.

"I'm good, just a bad day, that's all." I shake my head slightly and grab plates from my cupboard.

"Okay, I get it, let me know if you change your mind," he says as he empties the food onto the plates, and we lock eyes. He carefully pushes my bangs behind my ears and smiles. I mouth *thank you* without looking away from him.

"Alright, let's eat," he responds. We move to the couch and flip on a funny movie. Derek thinks that Adam Sandler is a sure way to cheer me up. He's not wrong. I'm tense as I sit on the couch next to him. I scooch back slowly to create more space between us. He doesn't notice. His eyes lock on the TV screen. After a while, I forget everything. I finally got a break.

My phone buzzes twice in a row.

Levi: *hey*

how are ya?

I smile and open the thread to text him back.

Me: *im good you?*

Levi: *rough day ngl*

Me: *you ok?*

Levi: *better now that i'm talking to u*

I was starting to think i scared you off after last night

Me: *nah you just set the bar too high*

now regular nights feel boring

Levi: *guess i'll have to raise the bar again then*

next time i'm adding hot chocolate and better music

Me: *better than the playlist last time?*

that wont be hard to beat

Levi: *woww*

you held my hand when Fleetwood Mac came on, that counts for something

A smile creeps across my face as I tuck my knees up to my chest. I look at Derek. He's distracted. He doesn't realize I'm not watching anymore.

Me: *true*

very bold move

Levi: *you didn't let go*

so i took that as a win

Me: *i didn't want to*

Levi: *next time, i might not wait so long to grab it*

Me: *guess i won't stop you*

Levi: *;)*

I smile and turn my phone off as the movie is nearing the end. I can't stop thinking about him and our night last night.

The movie ends, and Derek sighs, "Alright, well, I'm gonna head out, I think. I'm tired," he says, getting up.

"Oh, okay, that's fine," I say, still sitting on the couch.

"Goodnight, Sadie. I'll see you tomorrow," he says, grabbing his stuff to leave.

"Goodnight, Derek," I say as he slips out the door. As soon as he leaves, I whip my phone out and pull up Levi's Instagram and scroll through his pictures. From pictures of him with a cow to pictures of him holding a nasty-looking fish. He's got this soft face that you could recognize everywhere. I open our texts again.

Me: *do you always hold girls' hands under the stars or am i just special?*

I stare at the message for a second before hitting send. I immediately roll over and bury my face in my pillow and let out a muffled scream. I cannot believe I just sent that to him.

Levi: o*nly when the girl's wearing a leather jacket*

so yeah

i'd say you're pretty dang special

Me: *mm smooth talker*

Levi: *nah just being honest*

i like being around you, Sadie

I smile and kick my feet against the couch.

Me: *want to be around me this weekend?*

Levi: *for halloween? absolutely*

I put my phone down and cover my face with my hands. Who knew I'm such a flirt? Part of me feels guilty for texting him like this when I was just hanging out with Derek. But Derek is just a friend. He's made that pretty clear. If he doesn't want me, then I don't want him.

Not anymore.

15

~disguised

I wander around the farmers' market a few miles into town. It's crazy busy this time of year. I have a small tote bag filled with fruits, veggies, and some pastries I found. They look delicious. I'm just killing time this morning. I even found some cute handmade coasters that would match perfectly in my apartment.

October is almost over, and I am not happy about it. My favorite month, filled with everything I love, is almost over. But my favorite fall-scented candles will never be out of season. There's still Halloween. One of my favorite holidays. You can disguise yourself. Hide from what you're dealing with. Pretend you're someone or something else.

Back in my apartment, I already made my latte, and it's sitting on my nightstand as I lie in my bed. I'm too comfortable to move or do anything now. I have my show on. I do this thing where I analyze every character as if I'm writing them myself. I'm deep in thought about the side character when Tess texts our group chat.

Tess: *what are we doing for halloween?*
Derek: *lets find a party*
Levi: *I have a friend at connecticut state lemme ask him*
Tess: *sadie?*
Me: *yeah im down*
Levi: *he invited us to his house for a costume party tonight*
Tess: *perioddd lets do it*
I swipe out of the group chat and open a text from Levi.
Levi: *r you excited*
Me: *meh parties stress me out but ill go for tess*
Levi: *you'll be ok i promise we'll be by your side all night*
Me: *okayyy*

* * *

I meet them in the lobby of the art building before we have to paint. Levi is the first one I spot when I walk in. He's standing next to Derek, leaning against the white wall on his phone, but puts it away when I walk in. He stands up straight and smiles, and I smile back at him. A real smile.

"Hi, Sadie," he says as I get closer.

"Hi," I say as Tess runs toward me and hugs me.

"Girl, where have you been?" she says, grabbing my shoulders and shaking them lightly.

"I've been busyyyy but I'm excited for tonight."

"I'm going as a sexy cat," Tess says loud enough for everyone to hear.

"Oh my gosh," Levi says, rolling his eyes before looking toward me, "what about you, Sadie?" he asks, looking toward me.

"I don't know yet, honestly," I say.

Tess face palms, "It's literally tonight."

"I know, I know. I'll figure it out," I say, laughing.

"We'd better get to work before Clara notices how late we are," Derek says, turning toward our room but still looking at me.

I nod, and Levi leans down to my ear to whisper, "Come to my room tonight, I have something for you."

I smile shyly and nod my head as he smiles and walks toward his room, looking over his shoulder back at me. I see Derek look at me quickly, but then look away.

"Um, what was that about?" Tess says as we fall behind the boys.

"Nothinggg I swear," I say.

"You're terrible at hiding things, but we can talk about this later," she says, laughing and walking away.

I enter our room quietly. Hesitating to go in all the way, so I stand in the doorway. This is complicated. I don't like complicated things. I walk up beside him and dip a brush into the deep brown, working along the outline of a root I sketched yesterday. I don't say anything.

We paint in silence, again. But not comfortably. There's something different about it today. Like there's something just under the surface for both of us, and neither one of us wants to be the first to say something about it.

"I still think your roots are better than my leaves," he says quietly. His voice is soft and gentle.

I glance over. "That's because I don't rush them."

"I don't rush," he argues, he smiles softly, "I'm just impatient," he says. I haven't seen him smile in a while.

"Same thing," I say, rolling my eyes. "They're important, you know. They hold the tree up when it's fighting the wind."

He breathes deep and turns slightly to face me. "You're kind of like that too, you know."

"Like a root?" I say, raising an eyebrow.

"Yeah," he says, "Steady. Even when you think you're not."

I look away, my brush still in my hand. "That's not what most people think of me."

"Well," he whispers, "maybe they don't know you like I do."

My breath catches. "Maybe, yeah," I say with a smile. He clears his throat and takes a step back. I pretend I didn't notice. Pretend my heart didn't skip a beat. We keep painting. Carefully.

But I swear, his hand brushes mine more than once. And I don't think it's by accident.

* * *

I look in my bathroom mirror at my last-minute costume. I threw together a green body suit that's skin tight under a white leather skirt. I saw the inspiration for a Buzz Lightyear, which is weird to say. I went to a party store and got these cute white goggles. My knee-high black leather boots match perfectly. And for once, I can't stop looking in the mirror. My hair falls down in loose curls, and I even put on some black eyeliner and green eye shadow. I rarely get ready anymore. Putting on makeup is exhausting.

"Dang Sades, you look hot," Tess says, walking into my bathroom in her 'sexy cat' costume.

"Thanks," I say. "I like your outfit too."

She smiles and shrugs. "I wish my boyfriend could come," she says softly.

"Me too, I want to meet him."

"You will eventually," she says. I put some gold hoops in and reach for my phone when it buzzes.

Levi: *u comin up here quick or what*

Me: *oh shoot yea one sec*

"Umm, I'll be right back, okay?" I say, rushing out of the bathroom.

"Uh, where are you going?" she says, following me out of the bathroom.

"Just Levi's room, quick," I say, partially under my breath.

"Ohh, okay for what?" she says.

"I don't know, he said he has something for me," I say, smirking.

"Mhm, okay, hurry up," she says. I nod and rush out the door up to his room. I knock on the door and swings open, and he's standing there in a Spider-Man costume. I can't help but a giggle squeaks out of me, and I cover my mouth.

"Stop laughing at me and get in here," he says, smiling. He grabs my arm and drags me into his apartment. I've never seen his apartment. Only part of his room when he FaceTimed me the other night. I look around when I walk in at his walls covered in posters of what look like national parks.

"You look good," he says, getting closer to me.

"So do you," I say, moving closer, trying to sound casual. Relaxed. His eyes go up and down my body like he's memorizing something. The air shifts between us. I feel like I'm moving more slowly. He raises his hand like he's going to touch my face, but then stops. I begin to lean in, just slightly.

But then I blink and he clears his throat. "You wanna see what I got you, or are you gonna keep staring at me like that?" he teases.

I laugh, "Shut up, Spider-Man." he laughs and moves into the living room. He grabs a small box from his coffee table and hands it to me.

"Here," he says with a smile. I look up at him and down at the box. I open it, and inside is a small metal lightning bolt key chain.

"I saw it the other day and thought of you," he smiles. "Lightning is unpredictable, strong, and kind of resilient, just like you. So you can put this on your keys to remind you of the resilient girl you are," he says as he shrugs and smiles, leaning toward me. I feel grounded all of a sudden. Like I'm where I'm really supposed to be.

"Oh my gosh," I say, taking it out of the box and placing it in my palm. "I love it, thank you," I say, looking up at him. He nods and grabs my keys out of my back pocket. I slip the key chain onto the ring and slip it back into my back pocket. I look up at him and rest my hands on my hips.

"I gotta get back to Tess in my room to finish getting ready," I say, not looking away from him.

"Okay, I'll see you downstairs in a little bit," he says, putting his hand on my back to guide me toward the door. I smile and do a little wave before slipping out the door back to my apartment.

"Are you almost ready?" I ask Tess when I walk back into my apartment.

"Yes, just about," she says, coming out of my bathroom. "What did Levi want?" she asks.

I pull my keys out of my back pocket and moved the other key chains to show her the lightning bolt. "He got me this," I say, smiling.

"Aw, that's cute," she says. I nod and tuck it away. "Are you still pretending like nothing is going on between you two?" she presses as she puts a hand on her hip.

"Fine, I like him, just a little," I say, sitting on my island stool.

"Mm, crazy cuz he likes you too," she says, sitting next to me.

"I just don't want to jump into something I'm not ready for," I say.

"I get it, take your time with it, Levi is sweet, he would never hurt you," she says, putting her hand on mine.

"I know," I look down at my watch. "Our Uber is almost here, we'd better get down there," I say. She nods, and we head down to the lobby.

I wave at the boys when we come down the stairs. Derek is dressed like a farmer. A very different look for him. Plaid shirt, worn jeans, and a straw hat that looks like it's seen better days. He even has a piece of hay sticking out of his mouth.

I raise an eyebrow. "Seriously?"

He shrugs with a grin. "Thought I'd embrace the aesthetic."

Tess snorts. "You look like you walked out of a Bass Pro Shop calendar." We laugh as our Uber pulls up to the apartments. Levi gets into the front, and the rest of us in the back. I'm forced to the middle seat between them, and my leg presses against Derek's. The contact jolts me a little. I try not to move or make it obvious. He shifts just barely. Tess is rambling about her outfit and what she plans on drinking, but I'm not really listening. I'm too aware of the curve of Levi's jaw in the mirror and how he is staring out the window. I see Derek glancing at me out of the corner of his eye.

"You okay?" he asks under his breath.

I nod quickly, forcing a smile. "Yeah, I'm good."

He nods and looks away.

My phone buzzes, and I pull it out but tilt it away slightly from Derek so he can't see.

Levi: *you're quiet back there*

Me: *just letting tess have her moment lol*

Levi: *or avoiding cowboy ken*

I bite back a grin and lock my phone. I stare out the window as we turn onto the freeway. I feel safe with them. With the three of them. Even if things are complicated or messy, I like being around them.

16

~ deafening

We pull up to a yellow house. It's dark out already, but the drive was short. We all file out of the Uber and stand on the curb staring at the house. The lawn is covered in Halloween decorations. We walk up the driveway as I pull out two drinks I brought for me and Tess. I hand her one, and she opens it before we even make it through the door.

"Where's mine?" Levi says, getting close behind me.

"Um, you don't like these," I say, turning to look at him.

"True," he says and laughs as he opens the door for us.

The place is covered in orange lights and cobwebs. I haven't been to a party like this in forever. Levi walks in first, and another guy walks up to him and gives him a bro hug. I can't hear what they're saying, but Levi motions to us, and the guy motions for us to come in. There's a beer pong table in the corner next to an entire table filled with liquor. It looks like your typical college house. I've always wanted to live in a college house. But I'm not sure if I'll ever get that opportunity. I finished two years of community college before coming here.

I really want to finish a Bachelor's degree at some point. But I feel behind.

Levi introduces us to a group of people who I think live at this house. I grab a solo cup and pour my drink into it. Tess makes friends with a couple of girls in the kitchen. She's social. I used to do things like that. I'm leaning against the wall when Levi slides against the wall next to me.

"You good?" he asks, leaning down to whisper it in my ear. I nod and look up at him, and give him a soft smile. He cocks his head like he doesn't believe me.

"Wanna be my partner?" he asks, looking toward the beer pong table.

"Sure," I say, walking slowly toward the table. When we get over there, I lock eyes with Derek from across the room. Some guy is talking to him, but it doesn't look like he's really listening. He won't look away from me.

Levi and I play for a while, but I'm not very good. He doesn't care. Every time I miss the cup, he just laughs. The other team won, obviously.

Levi leans down to my ear, "Wanna go find somewhere quieter for a minute? It's kind of loud in here."

I look around. The living room is packed now, Tess is standing by Derek, and they're talking. Well, Tess is talking. Doesn't look like she's letting Derek get a word in. I like that he's a good listener like that.

"Yeah," I say quietly. "Let's go." Levi gently takes my hand, his fingers barely curling around mine. We pass them, and I look at Tess as she raises her eyebrows at me. I roll my eyes and we weave through the crowd, down the stairs to the basement. There's an old, torn-up couch down there and a bean bag. He closes the door halfway behind us. He flops onto the bean bag, and I sit on the floor in front of him with my drink in my hand. I'm starting to feel it a little bit, but honestly, it's making me a little more relaxed.

"It's nice being here with you," he says, looking down at me.

I smile and take a sip out of my cup. I stare at him for a while without saying anything.

I take a breath, "I feel different with you," I say before I can stop myself. My voice is nervous but honest.

He moves to the end of the bean bag and sets his drink on the table next to us. I do the same. "Different how?"

I don't answer at first. I just stare at him. "I don't know," I finally say. "I can't describe it," I pause, "I feel like I don't have to pretend." I look at him with his arms propped on his knees.

Levi smiles slowly. "Then don't," he pushes my hair behind my shoulders. He grabs my hand and pulls me onto the bean bag next to him.

I turn to face him, "You know, when I came here I didn't want to make any friends, let alone catch feelings for someone."

"Who do you have feelings for?" he asks, smiling.

That's a good question.

I laugh nervously. "Oh shut up," I say, pushing him. He doesn't say anything else. He just looks at me. He places his hand on my knee, but I don't flinch. I don't move. I don't even look away. He places his other hand on my cheek and slowly leans in to kiss me. It's careful. Like we've been wanting to do it for a while. Everything seems calm, and I don't stop kissing him. His hands move to my lower back, and he pulls me in closer. I feel safe. Secure. Like when he's holding me, I could never get hurt.

But just for a moment, Derek flashes into my mind. It startles me. Levi, I remind myself. I like Levi. If he's what I want, then why am I still thinking about Derek? I shake the thought before it gets too deep. I am still kissing him after all. I start to run my hand through his thick hair when I feel my phone buzz in the waistband of my skirt.

"Sorry, it's Tess, I'd better answer," I say. He nods, but I don't move away from him.

"Hi Tess, what's up?" I say into my phone, still staring into Levi's eyes.

"Hey, our Uber to leave will be here in like 15, just so you two know," she says.

"Okay, I'll come find you in a few," I say softly and hang up the phone. "We'd better get going," I say to Levi, whose hands are still on my back.

"Mm, not yet," he pulls me back in. I roll my eyes and kiss him again and again. We finally get up, and he won't stop looking at me.

"You know how pretty you are," he says as I pick up my drink.

"Mm, no better tell me," I say, smiling up at him.

"You are very pretty," he grabs my arm to kiss me again.

"Alright, let's go," I say, opening the door to get back upstairs.

"Hi Tess," I say, coming up behind her. She whips around and smirks at me and Levi coming up the stairs.

"Oh, hi guys, our Uber is here," she yells over the music. She's clearly drunk.

"Where's Derek?" I ask, pulling the bottom of my skirt down.

"Um, I think waiting outside," she says. We walk out the front door after Levi says bye to all his friends. Derek is sitting on the top step, and he gets up when he hears us come out the door.

"Ready?" he asks, and we all nod. I watch as our Uber pulls up to the house.

"Are you okay, D?" I ask, placing my hand on his shoulder.

He turns around and looks at me for a second before responding, "Yeah, just tired," he says as he stops walking. "Are you okay?" he asks, glancing at Levi and back at me.

"Yeah, I'm good," I say with a smile. He nods and starts walking.

"Hey, um, do you want to go to Skippy's tomorrow or something?" I ask him.

"Yeah, that would be fun," he says, smiling. I nod and get into the Uber. I just kissed Levi, but that doesn't mean Derek isn't my friend. I still need friends. Especially Derek. He's sweet and thoughtful. He's always been there for me.

I look out the window. My reflection stares back at me as we go on the highway home.

I can't help but wonder if being close to one makes me think of the other.

What does that really say about what I want?

17

~ the gray area

O ctober ends with a screeching halt, and before I know it, it's November. My pumpkin spice latte is still out, and the leaves are starting to fall. It's hard to believe I've been here for almost two months already. I do feel like this is helping. Although our tree has a long way to go, I really like it. Clara told us we are presenting our murals before Christmas. Apparently, a bunch of important art people are coming to look at them and give out scholarships to the one they like the best. I can't lie, a scholarship is enticing. If I ever do decide to go back to college, it could help me. But I'll cross that bridge when I get there.

I move my laundry from my basket to my bed and carefully put my comfort socks away. I have my music playing from my little speaker, and I dance around as I put my laundry away. Levi likes to send me new bands or songs to listen to. I like that about him. He isn't afraid to show me how he feels about me. Some part of me does worry about him sometimes. He says he's doing well right now, but I know how dark depression can get, especially for those who seem to be doing well. All of us are healing and growing. I just have to keep an eye on him.

I told Tess I'd meet her at the coffee shop down the street before we have to paint. I've been so focused on other things, I forgot what my therapist said about friendships. She's been a great friend to me, and I owe it to her to be a good friend back.

"Hey girl," I say as I walk into the lobby.

She smiles and gets up from the chair, "Hey, you ready?" I nod and we walk to the coffee shop. I like that it's close to the apartments. Tess doesn't really like coffee, but she gets a chai tea usually.

"Soooo I've been dying to hear what happened when you and Levi disappeared," she says as we find a table. I look around to make sure there's no one here from our program.

I smirk and take a sip of my latte. "We, um, kissed on the beanbag in the basement," I giggle and set my drink down.

"Oh my gosh?" she says, almost spitting out her drink. "You're joking."

I shake my head. "Nope."

"Okay, give me the details. This was the first time y'all kissed, right?" she asks.

I nod, "Yeah, we were just talking, then he pulled me onto the bean bag next to him."

"Stop it right now," she says with her jaw practically on the ground.

"Okay, but that was it. We didn't do anything else."

"Alright if you say so," she says mockingly.

I look up and smile. She grins at me and we laugh. Not everything has to be so complicated.

"Don't tell Derek, though, okay?" I reply, hoping she'll agree.

"Okay... I won't, but why?" she asks, tucking her baby hairs behind her glasses.

"I don't know, he gets weird whenever I mention Levi." I adjust in my seat nervously. Talking about both of them together makes me anxious.

"Probably because he likes you, Sadie." Her head falls onto her right shoulder.

"There's no way. Don't you remember what he said in the bar?" I remember that night. How magical New York was, and how it all came crashing down in the bar. I was wrong about everything.

"Yes, but I've seen the way he looks at you," she says quietly.

"Like a friend," I say. I mean it. He treats me like a friend. Now he does anyway.

"What if he tells you how he feels?" she asks.

"He won't." That doesn't sound very convincing. Not that we have ever talked about anything like that.

"But what if he does?" she pushes, while looking me directly in the eyes.

I shrug, "I like Levi, so," I say with some confidence.

"Remember how you liked Derek, too?" she adds.

I sip my latte. "I never said that."

She hesitates, "It wasn't hard to see that even when we first met."

"Tess," I pause. "He's my friend, okay?" I try to sound as convincing as possible.

"Okay…" she grabs my hand, "just remember you're not the only one trying to heal here."

I nod, "I know." I do know. I know what they have both been through. The last thing I want to do is hurt them.

"If he's your friend, then you should be transparent with him," she says, sitting back in her chair.

"You want me to tell him I kissed Levi on a beanbag in a random basement?" I ask, laughing softly.

She rolls her eyes and laughs with me, "No, but maybe letting him know something might make it less awkward, you know?"

I nod. I understand what she means, but part of me doesn't want him to know. Maybe it's because he and Levi are friends, but maybe it's because I don't want him to lose interest in me. But that part makes me feel guilty.

We finish our drinks and start our walk back. It's getting cold, but my leather jacket still makes an appearance.

"I'm hanging out with Derek tonight," I say as we enter our apartment building.

She pauses, "Okay, are you going to tell him?" she asks hesitantly.

"Haven't decided yet," I push the elevator button.

"Does Levi know?" she asks, shifting her bag onto her shoulder.

"You're full of questions today, aren't you?" I say and laugh, "Levi knows we're good friends, he doesn't care."

"Alright, whatever, but when y'all get back, we're watching a movie in my room," she says, holding the elevator door open as she gets out.

"Nothing would make me happier," I say with a smile.

* * *

"When do you want to go to dinner?" I ask Derek, but not looking up from our mural.

"Like thirty minutes?" he says, pouring more paint onto his tray.

"Sure, then Tess wants to watch a movie," I say. He nods and continues to work on his section. I want to keep talking. I like to talk to him. Usually, it feels mutual, but not today. But on the other hand, our tree is beautiful. Who knew that two strangers with no painting background could create something like this? Something as strange and beautiful as a simple tree could be.

I stare at the brown trunk, accompanied by orange and yellow leaves above it. It needs more. More life to it.

"Do we have red?" I ask, getting up off my stool.

"Yeah, I think so," he looks up at me, and puts his brush down. "Where are you putting it?" he asks, helping me rummage through our bucket of paints. He pulls out a bright red. It's too bright.

"Dark red, for the leaves," I say, pulling a darker red from the bottom of the bucket. "Perfect," I step up onto my stool to be eye level with my leaves. I look behind me at him, standing right below me, looking at the leaves.

"Go for it," he smiles his bright smile at me. I nod and make big strokes of the dark red on top of the yellow and orange. It pops. It looks like an autumn tree before the leaves fall to the ground for them to be swept up. I look back at him again for reassurance in what I just did. There is no going back now.

I step down after a while, making the red look perfect with the orange leaves. The red is the extra I was looking for. It made the tree look unique and special to just me and him.

Me and him.

We wrap up for the day, but I'm happy with what we got done, and I think Derek is too. I run to grab a mop from down the hall to clean up the paint we spilled on the ground again. When I'm in the closet, I hear a familiar voice behind me.

"Ohhhh Miss Harperrrr," Levi sings in the hallway. I turn to face him and smile.

"Hi," I grab the mop and move out of the closet.

"So movie at Tess's tonight, right?" he asks, grabbing my hand.

"Yes, later I think," I let out a deep breath and shift my weight to my right leg.

"Want to get dinner before?" he asks, looking down at my hand.

"I can't," I say, avoiding his eyes. "Derek and I are going to Skippy's if that's okay?" I say cautiously. He doesn't seem like the type to be mad, but you never know.

"Yeah, that's cool, I'll go get some treats or something," he smiles and starts to walk back to him and Tess's room. "See you there," he drops my hand and fully turns around and disappears into their room. My heart starts to beat fast. My smile fades, and I go to mop up our spilled paint.

I put everything back as Derek grabs our stuff so we can go eat. The cold air hits my face, and my hair flies off my shoulders when we leave the building. The sun is already setting, but the sky is covered in pink and orange clouds. It's busy, but there's always room for us.

"We should eat quickly before Tess chews our heads off for being late to movie night," he says, glancing at his menu.

"True, but it's okay, we have all night," I say, grabbing a straw for my water.

He smiles, "This coming from the same Sadie who used to always be in her apartment by 9 p.m." he laughs and shakes his head.

"Hey, people can change," I giggle and lock eyes with him, but he looks away. "I guess I'm just learning to live a little more," I shrug and set down my menu. I already know what I want. A grilled cheese with some fries. My go-to now when

Derek and I are here.

"Good," he says and smiles. I missed his smile.

We eat and talk about our mural. He tells me about what his sister has been up to and shows me a picture of her playing flag football. "She takes after me," he says, looking at the picture with pride. He's so proud of her. "You have an older brother, right?" he asks, setting his phone down.

"Not a good one," I roll my eyes as I finish off my fries.

He cocks his head, "Why?" he asks, looking up at me.

I shrug, "he bailed on me when I really needed him." I breathe deep, picking at my crust. "When everything got bad, he was nowhere to be found." I pause and take a deep breath. "He knew what I was dealing with, he could've stepped in, shown up when I said I needed help, but instead, he pretended not to know anything since my ex was his friend." I look down and quickly tuck my hair behind my ears. "He chose his friend over my safety," I finish.

He looks deep into my eyes. "That was selfish of him," Derek says without hesitation. "He should've protected you," he breathes in, "I would do anything to protect June, you deserved that too."

I nod and finish my water. It makes the gurgling sound as the ice moves around my straw.

"We should get to Tess's," I say with a smile.

He nods. "Agreed, she scares me," he laughs. He pays our bill again and holds the door for me as we leave. The walk to the apartments is quiet but a better quiet. Not an awkward quiet anymore. As we enter the lobby, his energy shifts.

"Something on your mind?" I ask him, looking at him walking on my right. He shakes his head and looks straight ahead. "D c'mon, what's going on?" I say getting into the elevator.

The elevator door shuts. He turns to me, "Are you dating Levi?" he asks.

I hesitate, unsure of what I should say. I know the answer. I look at him, but he's avoiding eye contact and looking anywhere else.

"Um," I pause and bite my lip, "no, I'm not." I glance at the ground and back up at him. He nods and fidgets with his keys.

"You don't have to lie," he says, finally catching my eyes.

"I'm not Derek," I take a deep breath. "We're not dating," I say. I'm not lying. But I guess it isn't the full truth. He hasn't asked me to be his girlfriend, but we like each other. I don't know if that constitutes dating. The elevator dings, and we get out on Tess's floor. We walk slowly in silence.

Before I can say anything else, Tess's door swings open, and she's standing there with a drink, and I spot Levi on the couch.

"Great, you guys made it!" She says and pulls me in. I look at Derek as she drags me in, and he follows slowly behind us. I need to clear the air, but I can't. I don't even know what to say.

Derek sits next to Levi, and they talk. I don't know how he's doing it. Just talking to him.

I sit across from Tess, pretending to laugh at something she says. But my eyes keep drifting to Derek. He's smiling, but not at me. Levi is on the floor again. He looks up at me as I'm staring into the distance, disassociating. "You good?" he mouths to me. I smile and nod to make it believable. But I'm still thinking about my unfinished conversation with Derek.

And I have no idea if I just lost him or if I ever really had him at all.

18

~ cracking

L evi's sitting on the edge of the stone fountain toward the back of our apartments. I spot him on my morning walk, which I take every once in a while. Fresh air has become essential in my routine. The fountain is running quickly behind him, and he has a notebook perched on his lap, pen moving steadily across the pages.

Our "campus" is quiet in the mornings. There's a soft hum of sprinklers in the distance.

"Are you writing about me again?" I ask, peeking over his shoulder as I approach him slowly.

He turns around when he hears my voice, "Wouldn't you like to know?" he smiles and closes his notebook.

I sit next to him and fold my right leg on top of my left. He turns and just looks at me.

"I like your outfit," he smiles. I'm wearing my favorite kind of fall outfit. My brown slippers, wide-leg jeans, and an oversized hoodie. "I wear this like every day."

He smiles, "I know, I like it," he says. We sit quietly, looking around at the many trees. I'm taking inspiration for our tree. And there it is. Derek. In my mind again. Remembering our conversation from last night. I lay awake in bed all night trying to figure out what I'd say when I saw him today. And I still don't have an answer.

"What was going on with you and Derek yesterday? Did something happen?"

I don't know in what way he means that, honestly.

"Um, yeah, I guess," I pause, looking at him. "He asked if we were dating," I say slowly.

"Oh," he hesitates, "what did you say?" he asks. He always speaks to me in his gentle tone.

"I told him no…" I look away from his bright green eyes.

"I mean, you didn't lie," he says, shrugging his shoulders. Ouch? I think.

"Regardless, things are weird between us, and I need to figure out why," I say, crossing both my legs.

"I mean, yeah, you guys are like best friends," he says. There's that word again.

Friends.

Derek is my best friend. He's been there. He's steady. Up until now, we haven't had problems. Which is why I need to fix things. I've always been taught how to be a good communicator. Especially after everything that's happened. I have to communicate my needs, or they'll never be met.

"Right, yeah, we just need to talk," I reply.

He nods and shifts his notebook on his lap. "I'm sure he'll be fine," he says, starting to get up. "Well, I need to go shower, but I'll see you later, okay?" he smiles. I nod, and he softly kisses me on the forehead. I watch him walk away in his special boots and Carhartt everything. He and Derek are polar opposites when it comes to clothing. Levi is from a small town in Maine. He doesn't like the city, he says. Too many people make him claustrophobic.

* * *

I've been so focused on my "new" life here that I've forgotten about what I do have at home. I have completely ghosted Julia. I saw her post solo pictures on Instagram from our favorite spot and realized I haven't reached out. My gut churns. I know she won't be mad, but that doesn't make me feel better. I pick up my phone and click her contact. After a few rings, she does pick up.

"Hi, Sadie," she says softly into the phone.

"Hi Jules, what are you up to?" I ask nervously, afraid she'll chew my head off.

There's a pause. "Just got back from work. I was about to go for a walk." Her tone isn't angry, but it's careful.

"I saw your post, you looked good," I say quickly, biting my lip.

"Thanks," she says. Another pause. "It was weird being there without you."

"I know. I'm sorry. I've been really caught up here. That's not an excuse, but it's the truth." I say, hoping she'll understand. She usually does.

She exhales on the other end. Not dramatic, just tired. "I figured. You're healing, it's okay."

I nod even though she can't see me. "I just—this place, it kind of flipped my world upside down. And I wanted to believe that starting over meant not looking back. But that's not fair."

She's quiet for a second. "I get it."

"I miss you," I whisper.

"I miss you too." Her voice is heartfelt. "I'll see you at Thanksgiving?"

I smile softly, "Obviously."

I tuck my phone in the back pocket of my jeans. I stare from my balcony. I feel like I've been running away from things. Or running toward the things that aren't right for me. It's hard to imagine where I would be if I were still at home. But this is my new home. For now, anyway. How can one place feel like home but foreign at the same time? The world keeps moving and spinning even when you don't want it to. Even when you'd rather stay in one place or be stuck in one moment. But the harsh reality is that you have to keep moving. Regardless of how much you want to stay put.

I need to figure out what to say to Derek. I need advice, but no one knows everything but me. No one knows what's under the surface. That's what makes it difficult. I know I need to be honest with myself. Things are moving fast with Levi. Too fast for what I'm comfortable with. I need to talk to him, too. But what am I even supposed to say?

I see Levi walking out of the apartments. I smile and pull my phone back out and click on his contact. I put the phone up to my ear and watch him pull his out.

"Hellooo Harper."

"Hi, turn around and look up," I say. He does just that and waves when he sees me. He stops walking and just stares up at my balcony.

"Guess what I did," I say confidently, smiling at him.

"What's that?" he says.

"I'm going to tour Connecticut State this weekend," I say. I filled out a tour thing last night. I figure I need to start taking control of my life. I want to go back to school, and I really do like this area. It might be right for me, so I have to see it out.

"Ohhh, that's dope, Sadie, it's a good school," he pauses, "can I come with you?" he asks, still looking at me from the ground.

"Preferably, so I don't get lost."

"Sounds like a plan, just text me when you're going," he says, starting to walk backward down the sidewalk.

"Okay, I will, good luck painting," I say and wave as I turn around to go back into my apartment.

"Good luck talking to Derek," he says. My smile starts to fade.

"Oh, thanks," I say. I can see his faint smile as he hangs up the phone. I grab my stuff and leave. I don't feel like painting. Sometimes it's just exhausting, and I'd rather do anything else.

* * *

"Hey," I say, walking slowly in the room, careful not to startle him.

"Hey," he says, looking up from his phone.

"How are you?" I ask, sitting across from him.

"Good, you?" he replies, locking his eyes with mine.

I nod, "Good." An awkward silence falls between us again. "I'm sorry about yesterday," I say as I fill my palette with my normal colors and try not to look at him.

"For what?" he asks. I look at him, confused because did he forget or something?

"Um, never mind," I say, grabbing some brushes.

"Look, Sadie, it's not a big deal, it's all good, okay?" he asks, looking back down at his phone.

"Okay."

113

I glance up at him. He's painting now. Working on the ground around the tree stump.

"You're my best friend," he says, smiling, "nothing could change that." He turns back around to finish the grass. I smile at him and nod.

Best friends.

We both go back to painting. It's no longer uncomfortable. Derek and I are like that. Comfortable enough with each other even when situations like this happen. He's steady. Predictable.

"Are you doing okay, though?" I say, turning toward him. Our faces are close together.

"Yeah, why?" he says calmly and pretty convincingly.

"Just making sure," I turn back to the mural and keep working on the sky background.

"You would know if something was wrong, Sades," he says with a smile.

"Right," I pause and turn toward him again quickly. "Can I have a hug?" I ask quietly

"Of course," he replies and stands up, helping me up to my feet before pulling me into a hug. He places his hand on the back of my head and rests his chin on the top of my head. We don't move for a little bit. I guess we both needed that hug. He pulls away and smiles. "Back to work, girl," he says, grabbing the paints.

"Yes, sir," I say, doing a fake salute. We laugh, and it finally feels like the air has been cleared between us.

* * *

"Hey, I'm going to see if Tess and Levi have this brush I want to use."

He just nods without looking up at me. I go down the hall toward their room, looking at my phone. As I turn the corner into their room, I see Levi on the ground in the corner and Tess crouched down beside him.

"What's going on? Is everything okay?" I say, rushing to crouch by Tess. Levi is clutching his chest and breathing really fast. His eyes lock with mine. They're wide and full of fear. He looks at Tess and shakes his head. I grab his knee.

"It's okay, just breathe," I say, looking at him, taking a deep breath myself. He copies my breathing and closes his eyes. We sit in silence for a minute.

Anxiety attacks. They are all too familiar.

"I'll be right back," Tess says, getting up and leaving.

His breathing eventually slows, "I'm embarrassed," Levi says.

"Don't be, it's okay," I say, sitting on the ground now. "Did something happen?"

"No, it just happens every once in a while. Most of the time out of nowhere," he says, putting his hand on mine. I nod, and we sit in silence again. He seems to know how to handle it. Which is sad to me. But I'm in the same boat. After a while, we become immune. Or at least be able to ignore it. But sometimes, it's impossible.

"You're okay," I say, still sitting beside him. He nods, and Tess comes back in with a water bottle. I look at their mural. It looks so good. They look like they've gotten as much done as we have. We will present them in about a month. Right before Christmas.

I help Levi up to his feet, and he gives me a quick hug before sitting in his chair. Tess hands me the brush I was looking for and hugs me, too. I ruffle Levi's hair carefully. "I got to get back, but game night in my room tonight?" I ask gently.

"For sure," Levi says, looking at me. He looks exhausted. Like he just got the life sucked out of him.

19

~ lurking

We sit around my coffee table on the floor playing a game of truth or dare. Cranberry spritz cocktails all around, perched on the coasters I got at a farmers' market last week. I lit one of my favorite fall-scented candles in the middle of the table. The best part of fall is using cute string lights and the glow of a candle over the big apartment light, any day.

Derek throws his head back, laughing at whatever Levi just said. I chuckle too, but not too loud, so it wouldn't be annoying to them. I'm comfortable with them, but it will take me time to completely come out of my shell. The shell that was placed on me unwillingly. But I can tell it wants to come off.

"Truth or dare, Sadie?" Tess looks at me and sips her drink.

"Truth," I smile and set my drink down on my coaster.

She nods, "Do you believe in love at first sight?" she asks, staring into my eyes.

I nod slowly, "I think so." I look up and see Derek looking at me with a small smile on his face. When we make eye contact, he looks away. "Okay, next," I start, "Derek, truth or dare?" as I turn to him.

"Dare," he replies.

I nod, "Hmm, I dare you to prank call the last person you called," I say, smiling.

He nods and pulls out his phone. He clicks a few buttons and holds the phone up to his ear. Two seconds later, my phone starts to buzz, so I pull it out of my pocket. His name lights up my screen. I roll my eyes and show my phone to them. We all laugh, and I decline his call. The laughter settles, and Tess grabs a bowl of popcorn and sets it in the middle of the table. "Okay, Derek, your turn."

He nods and turns to Levi, "Truth or dare, Mr. Levi?"

"Truth."

Derek rubs his hands together, "What's the dumbest thing you've ever done?"

Levi laughs and thinks for a moment. "Okay, okay, when I was like 15, my brother and I decided to race down the hill in our neighborhood during the winter. I was winning and looked behind me, and I hit an ice patch on the hill. I fell headfirst and scraped up my face and broke my arm," he says, laughing.

My stomach churns, and I start to sweat even though it's cold in my apartment. The room feels smaller, like the walls are inching closer.

I turn wide-eyed, hoping I lost him. I didn't. He's close behind. I can feel his breath as he tries to take mine. His rough hands take hold of the back of my neck. My mouth is wide, but nothing is escaping from it. Fists clenched, I open my eyes to see the sky. The ground slips out from underneath me. As my head strikes the pavement, darkness envelopes me, swallowing me whole.

118

I get up and sprint into my bathroom, covering my mouth as panic surges through my body. "Sades, you okay?" I hear Derek behind me. I don't answer. I hardly get the door shut and the toilet seat up before I vomit into the toilet. I sob softly, thinking it was over, but it wasn't. It replays in my head over and over again as I continue to throw up. I hear a knock on the door. "Sadie?" Derek's voice echoes through the door. I sit on the ground for a minute, not sure if he's still outside the door. I try to forget it, but it plays on a loop in my mind, that night, that fall, that sound of my own scream, waking up in the hospital. I choke on it like it's still stuck in my throat.

I flush the toilet and stand up slowly, breathing deep. "I'm fine, I'll be out in a sec." I grab my toothbrush and spit everything into my sink. Cold water hits my forehead, and I tap a towel against it to dry.

I open the door slowly and see Derek still standing there. He looks up from the ground. "Are you okay?" he asks.

I nod, "Yeah, I think my drink wasn't sitting right." I smile and start to walk by him. He grabs my hand before I can push past him and raises his eyebrow at me because he knows I'm not telling him the truth. "I'm fine, Derek, seriously."

He nods slowly and follows me back to the living room. "Okay, where were we?" I smile and pour myself some water from my pitcher and sit back down on the ground. They all stare at me like they've seen a ghost. I smile, "I don't think I ate enough today." I shrug and sip my water.

"Let's go get something to eat then," Levi says, getting up.

"I agree you should eat." Tess gets up too.

I don't stand up. "It's fine, guys, I'll get something later."

Derek also stands up, "Not happening." he reaches down for my hand and helps me back up. "I'll drive."

We grab our things, ditch the cocktails, and hit the nearest taco place with a drive-through. Derek lets me sit shotgun, and I stare out the window as we drive across town. The closest one is fifteen minutes away. I tried to insist we go somewhere closer, but Derek just shrugged and started the car.

The drive-through is slightly busy. Maybe like four or five cars ahead of us. Derek knows that eating in restaurants stresses me out, so he offers the drive-through for all of us. Sometimes it's difficult not to feel like a burden around them or that I'm too needy. But they don't mind. Derek doesn't mind adapting to my needs if it means I do things with them. Julia sometimes gets me like that, but it can be hard for her to see my perspective. It takes a special group of people to break open my shell.

The smell of tacos and hot sauce floods Derek's car once we've gone through the drive-thru. The drive back is quieter than it was on the way there. I watch the blur of streetlights pass the window. Derek turns the heat up a little. I hadn't said anything, but I'd been rubbing my arms. No one says anything about earlier, and that makes it easier for me to breathe.

We make our way back to my room and eat on the floor around the coffee table again. The deck of cards was still spread out from when we played Go Fish. We're not the kind of group to eat in silence. But for a while tonight, we did. I could tell everyone is exhausted from painting and doing whatever else we like to do. We had left a movie playing beforehand, so we just watch it instead of forcing conversation when clearly none of us are feeling it.

"Want us to hang for a bit?" Tess asks as I throw away all our garbage and take it out of the can.

I shake my head. "I think I just need to crash."

She nods, brushing crumbs off her shirt. "Text us if you need anything, okay?"

Levi picks up the bag of trash on his way out. "I'll take this out on my way down," he smiles.

"Thanks," I reply softly. Tess hugs me lightly before moving toward the door. Derek lingers, glancing at the candle I haven't blown out yet. He walks over and snuffs it with the lid. "Bye, Sades."

"Bye," I whisper and close the door behind them, pressing my back to it for a moment as the silence of the night creeps into my apartment. The string lights are still glowing, making me feel more comfortable with the silence. But it's hollow.

* * *

Sometimes I go stir crazy in this room. It's claustrophobic. Nothing I can do will make it feel like home. I do like it here, but something about it just doesn't feel like it's where I'm meant to be. But I still have time to figure it out. I used to love sitting alone in my room. I had many hobbies that I would switch between when I had free time. Reading, writing songs, strumming on my guitar, or playing Minecraft. Anything you could see me doing, I probably had done. I like that it keeps me busy. Even when I was in high school and taking AP classes and studying all the time. I always made sure I had time for my hobbies.

I had put my guitar in storage after a while. I thought about getting it out of storage when I came here, but figured I wouldn't use it. Now I wish I had. I find a beautiful guitar I absolutely love and order it to my apartment. It should be here after I go on my tour of Connecticut State. I maneuver away from my newly placed order and look up the school. I look through pictures, the campus, etc. It's gorgeous and I could definitely see myself going there. Since I have a bunch of generals finished, I would probably only have to be there for two-ish years. I am lucky, though, my parents are still willing to pay for me to finish school. I think this program is helping me realize that my life didn't end at 20. It's only the beginning.

I relight my candle and put a Sombr vinyl on my record player. It's a little scratchy, but it sounds nostalgic. It's calming. I sit on my couch and contemplate what I should do. It's only 9:00 and I don't want to go to bed yet. Derek has officially turned me into a night owl. I switch between socials and don't see anything interesting. Levi liked my story about the new song from his playlist. The one I made into a little collage of the four of us. Things between us have been off lately. I still like him, I know I do, but it feels like he's taken a step back, and I don't know why. I feel like I should know, but I don't know why I don't. I'm going to ask him when we go on the tour. Maybe I can get the clarity I've been searching for. And maybe that'll tell me what I want to know.

I open the door to my balcony for some air. The chilly breeze hits my face, but I have my jacket on. It's dark. Quiet. Lonely. But I have my notebook. Sometimes lyrics flow out of me, and sometimes they sit like a rock in the back of my head. Tonight is a night they flow out of me. Right onto that sheet of paper. I fill page after page, but not all of it is even coherent. But that's fine with me. I write about him if I'm being truthful. The time he took away from me. The trust in others he stripped from my hands. My confidence in myself and who I was becoming. Gone.

I notice my pen starts to shake in my hand, and I accidentally smear the ink across the page. I look down at my legs bouncing up and down. I start to heave through what feels like blocked lungs. My palms clam up.

Here we go again. My hand presses on my chest to remind myself I'm real and here. The pit in my stomach from earlier is still there, and I'm noticing it again. I close the notebook and slowly gasp for more air. Like it is being ripped from my lungs. I tell myself to breathe in, out, in, out just like I've been taught, like it's supposed to help. But right now, the oxygen tastes like guilt. Like fear.

Like him.

I realize that no one is coming to save me. I have to handle this on my own. I lay on the couch, and the emptiness stirs in the air. But I don't have to be alone. I remember what my therapist said. To lean on those around me. I know that. But I hate to feel like I'm burdening them with more than they can handle. We're all struggling.

But screw it, I can't be alone.

With mascara stained under my eyes, I grab a couple of things like a charger, my stuffed animal, and a change of clothes. It's late now, almost midnight. I shut off my lights and close my door behind me. The elevator is quiet as it brings me up a level. I stand in front of room 306 and stare at the door before eventually knocking quietly. The door swings open, "Oh, hi, Sades," he smiles.

I stare at him for a moment. "Hi," I say slowly. He has his headset around his neck, and he's in his flannel pajamas. I've seen them in many Snapchats. I take a step forward and stop.

"What's wrong?" he asks, putting his phone in his pocket.

I hesitate, "Can't sleep." I take a deep breath and look into his eyes. Suddenly, I feel a little safer. "Can I crash here?" I ask, looking at the ground.

He grabs my hand and pulls me into his room. "Of course, you can."

I close his door behind me, "Thanks."

He smiles and grabs my bag off his shoulder. "You can take my bed. I'm going to be up playing my game anyway," he says, gently going into his room.

"Are you sure? I can sleep on the couch," I follow him.

"Yes, I'm sure," he gives me a half smile and goes back into the kitchen. I turn off his light and climb under his covers. He comes back in with a glass of water and sets it next to me on the nightstand. He hands me his remote to his TV that is mounted on the wall, "I know you hate to fall asleep in silence."

I turn the TV on to a random movie. "Thanks, D," I smile and lie down on his pillow. It smells like him. I pull the blanket up to my chin and look at him standing above me.

"One sec," he says, going into his bathroom. He comes back with a warm, damp cloth. He bends down to be eye level with me, "You just have some makeup under your eyes." He lightly wipes my skin with the cloth. My eyes are closed, but I can feel him looking at my eyes. "There." I open my eyes, and he smiles at me and pushes all my hair out from my face and behind my back.

"Thank you," I smile softly.

"Goodnight, let me know if you need anything," he says, turning to the door. I nod and close my eyes. I hear him shut the door behind him and resume his game. He's talking to his friends quietly, but I don't mind. The sound of his voice comforts me.

20

~ drifting

I wake up to the soft sound of the TV still on, some random movie playing. The light fills the room through Derek's brown curtains. Everything in here smells like him. That faint cinnamon scent he always carries without trying.

I see the water on the nightstand and a folded hoodie next to me on the pillow. He must've left it sometime in the night. I stretch under the covers, yawn, and glance around. I put his hoodie on, it's cold in his room, but I only brought a t-shirt. I wonder if he's up yet.

I quietly open the door and glance out into the living room. It's empty, so I wander out of the room. I walk to the fridge to fill up my glass, and I find a sticky note on the counter.

Went to the store- be back soon — D

I smile without meaning to. My chest doesn't feel so heavy this morning. For the first time in a while, I don't feel like I'm waking up from a nightmare. I sit on his couch with my glass and check my phone. Unread text from Levi last night.

Levi: *See u tmrw for the tour!*

Crap, I forgot it's today. I know we have to leave at noon.

It's already 10:00 and I need to shower, so I'd better get going soon. Part of me wants to wait for Derek to get back, but I don't know when that'll be.

Me: *meet u downstairs at 12*

I set my phone down and look around his room. It's tidy and organized. Not how you would picture a young guy's room, that's for sure. I scroll on my phone to pass the time waiting for him to come back. My hair is still thrown up in a messy bun with a bunch of pieces pulled out that lay on the side of my face.

Derek opens the door and smiles as he walks in, "Morning, Sades."

I sit up straight on the couch, still in his sweatshirt. "Morning," I smile.

He sets a few things on the counter and moves toward me, and hands me a warm latte and a bagel. "Figured you might be hungry."

I grab it out of his hands and take a sip. It's perfect. "Very," I start to eat the bagel. He got himself one too. They remind me of the ones we had in New York.

He sits next to me on the couch, but we don't say much. I break the silence, "I should get going soon, I gotta get ready."

He sets his coffee down on the table. "Okay, yeah, what are you doing today?" he asks.

I hesitate, afraid of what I'm going to say, "I'm going to tour Connecticut," I say slowly.

"Oh, that's cool," he pauses to think, "are you going by yourself?" he asks, like I knew he would.

I sip my coffee again, "Levi said he'd come with me," I say very slowly.

He nods slowly, looking away from me, "Ah."

I bite my lip, "Yeah, just because he knows people there, so I figured that would be helpful."

"Right, yeah, that makes sense."

The silence fills the room again. "Thanks for letting me crash here," I whisper.

He finally makes eye contact with me, "anytime," he pauses, "you're always welcome here," he finishes and smiles softly.

I stand up to collect my things. I already devoured my bagel. "I'll see you later?" I ask as I make my way out the door. He follows me to the door.

He just nods, "bye, Sadie," and closes the door behind me.

* * *

I walk down the hallway with my bag over my shoulder, Derek's tone still sitting quietly in my chest. Did I hurt him or upset him in some way?

Back in my apartment, I toss my phone onto the bed and head straight to the bathroom. My reflection is a little jarring. Circles under my eyes, makeup faintly smudged, hair still a knot. I tug it down and brush through it with my fingers. I stare at my reflection for a minute.

The water in the shower is slow to heat up. I don't wait for it, knowing I should hurry. I shouldn't take too long. By the time I'm dressed and new mascara applied to my lashes, my phone buzzes just as I'm tying my shoes.

Levi: *Be down in 10.*

I stare at the screen, then slip it into my pocket. Derek's hoodie perched on my couch, folded neatly, ready to be returned. But what if I didn't return it? What if it stayed there for just a little while longer?

One last look in the mirror, and I head out the door to find Levi patiently waiting by his truck. Just like he was the night we went to look at the stars. He smiles as I come into view. His hair brushed over his forehead. It's messy like mine was before I washed it. The way he carries himself is charming. Like he would always protect me if I ever needed it. He often disregards the things he deals with, which makes me feel for him. Hiding ourselves away and wanting everything to seem normal. But it's not.

I smile as I approach him.

"I see you upgraded your leather jacket to an actual winter coat, finally," he says, getting into his truck.

I roll my eyes and hit his arm as I climb into the passenger seat. "I'm cold, okay," I laugh at him.

The drive there isn't long. Reminds me of our night on Halloween.

"Are you going to join a sorority?" he asks, not looking away from the road.

I laugh, "Do I look like the type to join a sorority?"

He throws his hands up in the air, "You know not really," he says, smiling and looking over at me. "You know I was in a frat before I dropped out."

I raise my eyebrows, "Oh, really?"

He nods carefully. Seems like he doesn't want to talk about his frat.

"Why did you drop out?" I ask even though I think I already know the answer.

He sighs, "I was just trying to survive, but every time I thought things were getting better, I'd slip again." He puts on his blinker and turns into the guest parking lot. "Thought it would be better to come back to college when I figured out

128

my mental health a little bit more," he says, putting the truck in park.

I nod slowly, "Yeah, I get it." I pause and grab my purse. "We're all just trying to survive, I guess," I finish and smile sympathetically. We don't get out of the car right away. "Have you toured here before?" I reach to unbuckle my seat belt.

He hesitates, "not officially, but my friend showed me around last year." He opens his door and steps out. I do the same. The cold breeze hits my face. I exhale and see my breath in front of me.

"Did you like it?"

He nods, "Yeah, it's a nice campus."

"I'm excited to see it."

"Me too," he agrees as we move together down the sidewalk. It seems weird he hasn't kissed me since Halloween. Granted, it's only been like two weeks, but still, weird. I think normally I'd read more into it than I am. But he's kind of hard to read, so my guess is it doesn't have to do with me. Maybe he's going through it right now. But he won't tell me.

Since most people don't tour this late in the year, our group is just me, Levi, and the tour guide, who of course knows Levi. The tour guide looks familiar. I feel like I saw him at the Halloween party. They talk and catch up as we walk around campus. The sidewalk is just wide enough for the three of us to all walk side by side.

"This is the arts building," the guide says as we approach an old, rustic building with moss-covered red brick. It's beautiful.

"Are the writing classes here?" I ask, walking up the couple of steps that lead to the building.

He nods and opens the door for us.

"You write?" Levi asks. I feel like that's not new news. I've been writing. A lot. He saw me writing in my special place in our own art building. How does he not know that by now?

"Yeah," I say, thinking maybe he just forgot. He doesn't say much else to me. But goes back to talking with his friend. I look around the inside of the building. It's old and has cute little chairs and couches in the lobby. The classrooms are on the smaller side since it's not a big university. I'd be really lucky to come here. I think I love it already.

We get to see the common area where they have a coffee shop. The gift shop, too, where I got a hoodie. I carry it on my arm as we finish the tour with a couple of other buildings and the gym. This school is the perfect size, I think. Not too big where I'd feel overwhelmed, but not too small where I feel like I'd stand out too much.

I crack a huge smile when I see their quad where a minimal number of students are hanging out. But something tells me it's a lot busier when it's warmer out. I see myself sitting at one of these benches, reading my book, sipping on a latte.

"So what do you think?" Levi asks me.

"I love it," I pause and take a deep breath. "I'm going to apply when we get back," I say confidently.

He smiles and grabs my arm, "You should."

I nod, and we walk back to his truck when the tour is over. He's quiet. I need to know what's going on with him.

As soon as we get in, I blurt, "Why are you being so distant all of a sudden?"

His head falls back onto the headrest, and he turns toward me. "I'm sorry," he pauses and closes his eyes. "It's not you."

"Then what is it?" I ask impatiently.

He takes a deep breath, "I guess I just got scared."

Scared?

"Scared of what? Of being with me?" I say harshly. I need to tone it down. I can tell he's hurting.

He nods. I wasn't expecting him to agree with me. "We're both just so," he pauses.

"Broken?" I finish his sentence for him.

He nods again. Silence fills the air. "I don't want to hurt you," he says, rubbing his eyes with both of his hands. "And I don't want you to hurt me."

"You wouldn't. I wouldn't."

His hands fall back onto his lap. "You don't know that."

I look back at the front of his truck.

"Hurt people hurt people, Sadie," he says. I can't disagree with that. I did a lot of things to people I wasn't proud of after everything happened. "I like you, Sadie, but things started to move too fast," he says softly, taking a sip of his soda.

"I know," I close my eyes.

"You know?"

"Yeah, it kind of made me nervous, and honestly, I didn't know what to think about it all." I scratch my head and turn back to him.

"I'm sorry," he breathes deep as he adjusts his hat.

"It's not your fault," I say, resting my hand on his shoulder. He shrugs. "We could just take things slow?" I say, turning my whole body to him.

He nods, "Let's do it."

I smile and let go of his shoulder.

"But if things go sideways for either of us, we have to be honest," he says sincerely.

"I agree, our own health needs to come first."

"Okay," he pauses and shifts the truck into reverse, "let me take you to dinner tonight then."

I can't help but giggle a little bit. "I'd like that."

He smiles as we pull away from the campus. "How about the steak house downtown?"

"I've been wanting to try that place," I say, taking my beanie off to unveil my hat hair.

"Okay then."

"Okay then," I smile and look out the window.

The buildings are getting smaller and smaller as we drive away. But I can tell, I'll be back. Sooner rather than later.

21

~ temptation

"What are you doing tonight?" Tess asks right as I pick up her call. I just got back into my apartment. I think she was watching my location on Snapchat.

"Levi is taking me to dinner," I reply, putting my things away.

"Oh, is he now? I thought he was being distant?" she asks.

I hesitate. "He was, but we talked and decided to take things slower."

"Probably good," she replies. There's silence on the other end. "Where were you last night?" she adds. I feel like I'm about to get in trouble with the principal for skipping class. I don't say anything. "I know that wasn't your headboard girl," she finishes.

Caught.

"Um, I couldn't sleep, so I crashed at Derek's," I say slowly, afraid of her response. That's the thing about Tess. She's not afraid to tell you the blunt truth or what you need to hear. And I know that's what she's about to do.

"Sadie, you cannot be going on dates with one guy and sleeping in the other guy's bed," she says forcefully.

"He slept on the couch...?" I say cautiously.

"Sadie, you gotta decide," she continues.

"Derek's my best friend, okay?" I say defensively, "Just like if I crashed at your place," I finish firmly.

"But you didn't, you went to Derek's."

"His apartment is closer...?" I say weakly.

I hear her sigh on the other end. "Just be honest with yourself, okay?"

"I'm going out with Levi tonight, and I'll tell you how it goes later, okay, byeeeee," I say and quickly hang up as she says bye too.

I could sit on my couch and think about what she says, but I have a date to get ready for.

* * *

I search through my closet for something to wear. This steakhouse is nice, and I want to look good for him. I almost land on a leather skirt or something until I glance into the back of my closet. Lo and behold, my green dress. The strapless one that has a ballerina skirt. I know I didn't pack this. It was my mother. My mother actually snuck it into one of my suitcases.

I'm going to wear it.

I slip it on and stare at myself in the mirror. I don't hate it on me. I haven't worn this dress since my cousin's wedding a couple of years ago. *Chase* had gotten mad at me for wearing something too revealing. I danced all night anyway.

I grab my curling iron for some loose curls and do my makeup in the little mirror on the counter. Subtle, but enough to see a difference. Black heels to go with the dress, they're short but strappy and cute. I stare at myself in the mirror for a minute or two. Trying to decide if he would like this dress on me. I think it's worth a shot. I reach for my purse and lip gloss before I head out.

There he is again, leaning up against his truck. A new outfit this time. A button-down shirt and cargo pants. His hair is so long, like he hasn't gotten it cut since we got here.

"Hi, beautiful," he smiles as I approach his truck. "Guess you couldn't get rid of the leather jacket," he says, opening the door for me.

"Never," I say, getting in. He shakes his head and laughs. As we pull away from the apartments, I look up to the third floor and see Derek on his balcony. He watches as we pull away and goes back inside. My chest tightens.

* * *

The restaurant is nice inside, like I expected it to be. Dimly lit with waiters in uniforms with black ties. We get seated in a corner of the restaurant near the kitchen. Levi pulls the chair out from the table for me to sit and then sits down across from me. After looking at our menus for a while, he sets his down and looks at me. "What?" I say smiling.

"Nothing, I just like that dress on you," he smiles and takes a sip from his water.

"Thank you," I reply, taking a bite out of the pumpernickel bread. My favorite.

He looks at the drink menu and hands it to me. "You want a drink?" I shake my head and grab my glass of water. He nods slowly and sets the menu down again. The corner of it slides into the butter dish. But he doesn't notice.

"So…" he starts, then trails off. I nod like I'm waiting for him to finish the thought, but he just smiles awkwardly and glances around the restaurant.

Our waiter finally appears with his notepad. He introduces himself and asks if we're ready to order. I'm not. But I nod anyway.

* * *

We finish our dinner and he pays the bill. He doesn't hesitate, just pays it. A lot of our conversations are about painting. He asked how Derek was doing with the painting. Honestly, nothing meaningful. Nothing of importance.

He called me pretty again. I wish our conversations were deeper. I feel like I hardly know him. I don't know his favorite food or what motivates him. And he doesn't know that about me either.

There's only one person here who does.

* * *

Back in my room, I change into sweats. My guitar was delivered, and I was so excited to unbox it that I denied Levi's request to hang out in his room. It's obsessed with it. A deep oak color that reminds me of my other one. Just slightly different. I strum and tune it until I think it sounds good. I start working on a tune for the lyrics I showed Derek. I added some more to it a few nights ago. I set up my phone to record myself so I can hear how I really sound. Not horrible. But let's be honest. When it comes to singing, I'm my own worst enemy.

The sweats I'm wearing are new. I ordered them a couple of nights ago. Being alone here is not great for my online shopping addiction, clearly. It's a light brown color and has some random wording on it. But it's so comfortable.

After playing my guitar for a while, I'm craving a milkshake from Skippy's, so I think I need one. A little sweet treat never hurt anyone. I grab my purse and walk over. It's a nice night out. A crisp 55-degree fall weather. I have my headphones in, though, so people know not to talk to me.

I open the door, hoping it isn't busy here so I can get in and out quickly. I walk up to the counter and order my chocolate shake, and hear my name called behind me. "Sadieee," Derek says loudly from a booth. He's sitting alone, enjoying a burger, it looks like.

I wave at him quickly as the waitress starts talking again, "Here or to go?" she asks me.

I look back at Derek, "Here, please, at that table," I say, pointing toward him. She nods, and I pay for it.

I sit down across from him and smile softly, taking my headphones out. "All by your lonesome?" I ask him.

He laughs and nods slowly, "I was hungry and didn't feel like cooking."

I nod and steal one of his fries. "My new guitar came."

"Ohhh, how do you like it?" he asks.

"I love it," I say, sipping on my shake. "Want to come see it?"

He nods and pays his check, "Absolutely," he starts, "Can I play it?"

"Don't push it," I say and laugh. He rolls his eyes and sits back in his chair.

"New sweats?" he asks, looking me up and down.

I nod. How does he know it's new? Maybe it's because I only ever wear the same three pairs of sweats, and they're all ratty.

We walk back quietly, and I hear his feet dragging against the sidewalk. The cool air whips against my cheeks. I keep my hands in my pockets, pretending I'm not hyper aware of how close he's walking. I smile to myself, half lost in thought, and tuck a piece of hair behind my ear before he notices.

When we reach my apartment, I grab my new, beautiful guitar off its blue stand in the corner of my living room. "Here," I say, handing it to him.

He grabs it and sits on the arm of the couch. As he pulls the guitar onto his knee and starts strumming. He looks at me, "I like it."

I smile and hand him a pick. "Thanks."

He starts playing something familiar, and I pause to look at him.

"Is that... Bon Iver?" I ask, raising an eyebrow.

He grins without looking up from the guitar. "You said you liked this one last week," he pauses, "and I just happen to know it from my sister."

I bite my lip. "You remembered?"

He shrugs but keeps strumming.

I sit down on the rug in front of him, pulling my knees to my chest and looking up at him, still strumming. His brown hair falls over his eyes, but he doesn't seem to mind it. I watch him carefully, "You're not bad."

"I'm fantastic," he corrects, smiling at me.

There's a pause, and he looks at me for a second too long.

"What?" I ask.

"Nothing," he says. But the way he's looking at me says something else.

I nod and grab the guitar from his grasp. "I need to shower," I say, motioning for the door jokingly.

He laughs and heads toward the door. "I guess you're kicking me out?"

I smile, "I am suggesting you exit."

He opens the door, "Hmm, got it," he laughs, and shuts the door behind him.

I'm not going to shower.

Time to open back up my book I started earlier.

22

~ before we go

"Ohhh Sadieee," I hear a voice call out from below my spot, perched on the second level of the building. I put my book down and look over the little railing separating me from falling off. Derek is standing almost directly under me, looking up at me.

I smile and drop my shoulders. "Hi Derek."

He tilts his head to the left. "Hi, Sadie."

We stare at each other, and I take a deep breath. "Time to paint, huh?" I start packing my things.

He nods, "Vámonos, chica," and moves toward our room down the hall. I grab everything and hustle down the stairs, maybe fast enough to beat him to the room. I was too slow.

He walks in right before me. "Are you going home for Thanksgiving?" he asks while setting up our paints.

I nod. "Mmhmm. Are you?"

"Yes, my sister told me if I didn't, she was going to throw away all my Legos, so I guess I don't have a choice," he smiles.

I laugh at him, "You build Legos?"

He stares at me, "You don't?"

I shake my head and grab my favorite shade of green. We settle into our rhythm. The canvas of our tree stretches across the far wall, big and wild. The shape is finally right, and the roots twist deep into the ground, the trunk is wide, and the branches curl upward. I love the combination of rich browns and soft greens. I say this every time I look at the wall, but something is still missing. The leaves aren't quite what I want. It doesn't feel alive yet.

Derek steps back, eyes scanning the tree. "We're getting close," he says.

"Yeah," I reply, dipping my brush back into the brown. "But not quite."

A silence echoes throughout the room. "So when are you leaving?"

"I think I'm going to head out on the 18th."

Today is the 11th. One week until I go home and face everyone. I wonder if Jason will even make an appearance for Thanksgiving this year. I wanted to leave later and spend less time there, but Julia begged me to come home earlier since she'll be on break from school, and we can do all the things we love to do when we're together. "When are you leaving?"

He sighs, "Probably the 20th." I nod and watch him work on the roots some more. "I usually don't care for Thanksgiving, but I have more to be grateful for this year," he says.

"Oh yeah? Like what?" I ask hopefully. I'm hoping he says what I want him to say.

"This place," he takes a deep breath and turns around to face me, "you," he grins.

I smile and stick my bottom lip out slightly. "I'm thankful for you, too, D." I reach my hand out and ruffle his messy hair.

141

"Whatever, get back to work," he laughs and spins back around.

"Yes, sir," I pick my brush back up.

* * *

We run into Tess and Levi as we leave our room. Derek and I were still laughing at how he messed up, and we had to get white-out from Clara to fix it. Normally, the perfectionist in me would be mad, but it got fixed, so it's fine.

"So what are we doing tonight?" Tess asks, looking at all of us in the parking lot.

I don't say anything, but I look at Derek. He shrugs, "Movie at my place?" he says hesitantly.

Tess gasps, "Yes, yes, yes, we are doing that." She claps her hands together and keeps walking.

We approach our building, and the boys walk in first, but I grab Tess's arm before she can walk in too. "Hey, are you going home for Thanksgiving?" I ask.

Her face changes quickly. "Um, no," she mumbles.

"Oh, why not?"

"My brother is at a rehab center in Minnesota, so they won't be home till the beginning of December," she says, and her lip slightly quivers.

"Oh," I grab her arm, "Come to my house then."

Her shoulders drop. "No, Sadie, I couldn't."

"Yes, you could and you will," I smile, "I'm leaving the 18th."

"Are you sure?" she asks.

I nod quickly, "My parents will love you."

"Thank you," she grabs me and pulls me into a hug, and doesn't let go for at least thirty seconds. When she finally does,

142

I nod and open the door.

"See you at 8:00," I say, getting in the elevator. It closes as she walks away to her room.

Maybe I should've asked Julia first before I offered. But I couldn't let her stay here by herself. We all need each other.

* * *

I walk into Derek's apartment once more and glance at his bed, where I slept just a few nights ago. It's unmade and inviting. But I sit on one of his island chairs. The other two weren't here because it's only 7:45. I came early to sit with him, just us, even though we spent the whole day talking today.

He sets a Diet Coke and a glass of ice in front of me. I like to pour it myself and hear the ice crackle and fizz up. He pours himself one too. I watch as he cleans his kitchen and pulls my phone out when it buzzes in my waistband.

YOU'VE BEEN ACCEPTED is plastered across my screen when I open an email from Southern Connecticut State University. I let out a very dramatic gasp and stand up from my stool.

"Are you okay?" he says, picking up the hand towel off the counter.

"I got in!" I yell, "I got into SCSU!" I start to jump up and down.

"Shut up, no way," he says, running over to my side of the counter.

I show him my screen, and he holds out his arms in disbelief. "That's so great, Sades," he says, picking me up and twirling

143

me around in the middle of the kitchen. As he is about to set me down, his door opens, and Tess and Levi walk in.

"What's going on?" Levi says cautiously. Derek puts me down, and we both turn to face them awkwardly.

"Um-" I start.

Derek interrupts me. "Sadie got into SCSU," he exclaims.

Tess runs into the apartment to hug me. "That's awesome, Sadie. I'm so proud of you," we both shift from foot to foot as we hug.

"Thanks, guys," I say, smiling. I look at Levi, and he just looks at me.

"Congrats," he says almost under his breath. I nod at him. I'm confused. He was just touring with me and wanted me to get in, and now it's like he doesn't care about it at all?

"What movie are we watching?" I ask, grabbing my drink as we all move into the living room.

"Your choice, Sades," Derek says, handing me the remote. He sits right next to me, and I look at Levi as he glares at Derek. Now the room feels tense, but I don't think it's my fault. Tess must have noticed too because she looks at me and mouths, *"What was that?"* I just shrug and flip through the different movies on the streaming service.

"Derekkk the big light," Tess complains. Derek rolls his eyes and goes to turn on his LED lights and a lamp or two.

I turn on an old animated movie from when we were younger. Nostalgic.

Levi's been quiet, scrolling on his phone but not really looking at it.

"Did anyone else cry during this movie when they were younger?" Tess groans dramatically.

Derek smirks. "No, you're just dramatic."

"I am expressive," she corrects.

I laugh and take another sip of my Diet Coke. There's a pause. I notice Levi set his phone down. "Um…" he starts, then stops. His voice is low, he continues, "I went to see my doctor yesterday."

We all look at him. But no one says anything. I pause the movie so we can hear him better.

"They're switching my meds," he says simply. "The old ones haven't been working for a while."

Tess blinks rapidly. "Levi…"

He raises his hand quickly and waves her off. "I'm fine. Just felt like saying it. I don't know." No one says anything right away. The sound of the movie just plays in the background of all of our thoughts.

Then Derek replies, "That's good, man. That you're taking care of it," and he pats him on the back.

Tess scoots close to him, puts her arm around him, and leans her head on his shoulder for a second. "Love ya."

I don't say anything yet. Just look at him. I don't know what to say, but I reach over and grab his hand for a second. He gives mine a quick squeeze and lets go. I am a horrible person. I am a horrible person. Obviously, something was going on with him. Why am I so selfish sometimes?

23

~ the back road

My suitcase that was just shoved into the back of my closet now lies open on my bed with nothing in it. I stare at trying to decide what I need to bring home. At least a couple of nice outfits, one for dinner and one to go out with Julia. I promised her we'd go to a brewery or something now that we were both twenty-one. After throwing a good amount of clothes and shoes into my suitcase, I grab my things from the bathroom and pack my backpack with everything else I need.

There's a knock on my door as I'm in the bathroom trying to decide if I need to bring makeup. I should.

"It's open, Tess," I yell from the bathroom. "I'm almost done packing," I continue to scramble around my bathroom. We are supposed to leave in twenty minutes, but I'm not sure I'll be able to accomplish all my packing by then. I come around the corner to my kitchen.

"Hey, sorry, not Tess," Derek says, standing in my kitchen.

"Oh, hey," I stop in my tracks.

He smiles, "I just wanted to say bye before you left."

146

I nod and pack some snacks into my bag for the road. "Are you okay?" I ask. His hands are in his pockets, and he looks like something is bothering him.

"Yeah, no, I'm good, just tired," he paces around the counter like he has more to say.

"Okay, well, I'll see you when we get back," I smile at him and walk closer to him.

"Then it's grind time on our painting," he says, shaking his finger in my face.

I laugh and give him a quick hug. "Bye, Derek."

He opens the door, "Bye, Sades."

As he walks out, I hear Tess panting down the hall with her huge suitcase.

Derek passed her coming down the hall. "Dang, are you moving out?" he laughs at his own joke.

She slaps his arm with her free hand, "shut up." She walks into my apartment. "I'm ready."

I laugh at her being out of breath and drag my suitcase out of my room. "I need coffee," I say, turning off all my lights. She nods in agreement, and we drag our stuff out into the hall. Lots of bags for only a week. But you never know what you may need.

* * *

We go through the drive-through just outside of town for coffee. "We're taking the scenic way back. You'll love it," I reassure her, pulling onto the freeway.

"Okay, but we have to play a fall playlist for the vibes," she responds, grabbing my phone and shuffling a fall playlist.

I nod, "It's 37 minutes longer but so worth it this time of

147

year, I think," I say as I take off my left shoe and pull my leg up onto my seat. The comfort position when driving long distances.

"I'm in no rush," she says lazily, also taking her shoes off and sitting crisscrossed on the seat.

The highway turns to back roads, and soon we're winding through stretches of orange and red trees. Half of the leaves are already on the ground. The air in my car smells like coffee. Clean, cold air seeps through the vents from the outside.

After a while, she leans her head against the window. "Okay, yeah… this is definitely the right way," she says, not looking away from the window.

I nod, glancing at her, then back at the road. "It always makes me feel better."

She closes her eyes. "I think I needed this more than I thought."

I sigh heavily and pause, "me too," I agree.

* * *

"We're hereeee," I yell as we bust through the front door of my Vermont home.

My mom comes barreling down the stairs, "Finally, you're home!" she exclaims, wrapping me up in a hug. "And you must be Tess, it is so great to meet you." She grabs her and pulls her in for a hug as well.

"It's nice to meet you, Mrs. Harper. Thank you for having me. I really appreciate it," Tess says gently.

"Of course, you're welcome anytime," she smiles and yells for my dad.

"Let's bring our stuff to my room," I say, grabbing my suitcase. We go down the hall and toward my room. Out of his room, on his phone, comes Jason. I didn't think he'd be here. He almost runs into me and looks up from his phone.

"Oh, hi, welcome home," he says, giving me a side hug.

"Thanks," I say, pushing right by him into my room.

Tess shuts the door behind her. "What was that about?" she asks.

I flop on my bed. "Don't you remember me telling you about my horrible brother?" I say covering my face.

"Ah, yes," she flops next to me. "Sorry."

I roll over, "don't worry about it. I thought he'd be some-where else, but I guess not," I say, looking at her. A silence falls over my room. My music posters still hung on the wall from before I left. My hanging chair still has an unfolded blanket on it. The chair is what I miss the most about my room here. It was comforting to read and ignore the world for a little while. "I told Julia we'd meet her for dinner tonight," I continue.

Tess sits up. "I can't wait to meet her."

I smile and start to unpack some of my stuff. There's a knock on my door. "Come in," I say, looking down at my clothes.

Jason walks into my room slowly. I look up at him and back down without saying anything. "Can we talk?" he asks without coming all the way into the room.

I take a deep breath, "Not right now, we're going to dinner," I say, still not making eye contact with him.

He opens the door a little more, "after?" he questions again.

I shrug, "Maybe." Tess is on her phone, minding her own business.

"Okay, have fun at dinner," he says, closing the door.

Tess slams her phone on the bed and opens her mouth, but

149

before she can get her words out, "don't," I say, holding my hand up and laughing at her. "I know what you're going to say."

"Great, then I don't have to waste my breath!" she smiles, "whatever it is, just fix it." She grabs her purse and looks at herself in the mirror. "Let's go," I nod and follow her out the door.

* * *

We meet Julia at our favorite restaurant in the downtown area. It's always packed, but she never forgets to make a reservation. Something I can't remember for the life of me. I just show up and hope we can get in. Our favorite thing to do is sit on the patio in the summer, but it's too cold for that now, so a booth by the bar should do. I don't see Julia until she runs up behind me and hugs me. Being with her is always so refreshing.

"Julesss, I'm so glad to see you," I say, hugging her. "This is Tess," I hold out my arms to her.

Tess pushes her black straightened hair behind her shoulders and goes in for a hug. "It's so good to finally meet you."

They pull back, and Julia grabs both of her shoulders. "Thanks for taking care of my girl in Connecticut," she smiles at her.

"Always," Tess replies, grabbing both of our hands.

They call Julia's name, and we make our way to the booth. It's a dimly lit restaurant with those big bulb string lights dangling from the ceiling. I order fish tacos, Julia gets crab cakes, and Tess goes out on a whim to try a lobster roll. I don't like them. They're cold and taste stale, but to each their own.

"So, how's the painting coming?" Julia asks. She sits next to me and Tess on the other side.

"Good, I think," I say. "Derek is actually not bad at painting."

"Neither is Levi, surprisingly," Tess adds.

Julia looks at her, "Wait, you're partners with Levi?" she asks. Tess nods and sips her Dr. Pepper. "The same Levi that Sadie made out with at that party?" Julia continues to pry.

"Yep, that's the one," Tess says, laughing.

Julia turns to me, "Are you still talking to him?"

"Yes, I am," I interrupt what feels like a conversation between the two of them about me.

"Oh, I could've sworn you'd get with Derek by now," Julia continues and smirks at me.

"Oh my gosh, Julia," I scold, "I like Levi." I cross my arms and let out a dramatic huff.

"Right, okay," they both say at the same time.

I roll my eyes, "You guys suck," but I laugh at the same time.

Tess puts her drink down. "She can't see that Derek is in love with her."

"Because he's not, for the millionth time," I say, looking at Tess.

"I've never met him, and I have only seen Instagram posts, but that man does not look at you like just a friend," Julia says in her usual sassy tone.

I shrug, "Well, it's not my fault he never made a move."

"Maybe because he knew you just got out of a traumatic situation," Tess says. Julia points at her in agreement.

Our waitress comes around the corner with our food. "Whateverrrr next topic please."

"Fine," they both say in unison. Tess continues as they set our food in front of us. "But, when it gets messy, I get to say I told you so." She looks at me with that face she does when she

151

knows she's right. There hasn't been a time when she wasn't. I nod and pick up a taco and shove it into my mouth. Delicious as they always are.

24

~ frozen ground

For the next few days before Thanksgiving, the three of us do as much as we can together. The mall, bowling, etc. Tess and Julia get along really well. I was worried that it would be this battle of the best friends thing, but it really feels like we are a trio.

I stalk Jason's location before I go home to ensure he's not there so I can continue to avoid the conversation he's been wanting to have about who knows what. Actually, I could probably guess it would be one of two things. Both of which I don't feel like talking about with him. But I can't avoid him forever, especially on Thanksgiving.

Jason and I used to dress up as turkeys for our little cousins on Thanksgiving and play with them all day. Now they're grown up and don't come to Vermont anymore. Their parents are wealthy and live on the beach in Maine. They're too cool to come here. It's upsetting, I really liked them. They were like built-in best friends, and I never had to try to be someone different around them.

Jason and I are Irish twins. He's only 11 months older than me. So we grew up basically like twins. We are in different grades, though, so once we got to high school, it was a whole other story. He got in with the stoners and skaters. I made my way to the book girls who would go to the library after school. After the first two years of high school, he would hardly say hi to me in the hallway anymore. Just brush past me and pretend that I was invisible, like everyone else did.

I was sitting alone at lunch one day because my friends were on the regular history trip that the AP kids didn't get to go on. I didn't mind it, it was nice to just eat in peace and crack open a good book. I had looked up, and this guy in a gray sweatshirt got up from Jason's table and sat right next to me at my table. I was confused because why would one of Jason's friends be sitting with his loser sister, who reads at lunch? He talked to me like he knew me. Like he saw me.

That's how I fell for him. He didn't always see me as something easy or a punching bag. He loved me at first. For who I was. But that *love*….

Turned to *hate*.

* * *

Thanksgiving finally rolled around. Julia went to her grandparents' house in New Hampshire for dinner. Tess and I got ready in my room. I pulled my cream knit sweater over my brown leather skirt and put on my black Doc Martens in case we leave the house. Tess had tried these overnight curls on my hair, but they didn't turn out great. I kept them anyway because I'm lazy and don't really care. Tess has great style. She wore a white tank top with a brown cardigan, with one side slipped off her shoulders. Her ripped wide-leg jeans perched perfectly over her Adidas Sambas.

"You look so pretty," she says as I put my gold hoops in.

I look at her in the mirror. "So do you."

"I'm starving, I can't wait to demolish some stuffing," she says.

I laugh and open the door to my room. The wonderful Thanksgiving dinner smell fills my room.

"Hey, um, Derek texted you," she says, picking my phone up off my bed and handing it to me. Of course, she reads what it says first and smirks at me.

Derek: *happy thanksgiving sades, grateful to be your friend*

I smile and start typing a response.

Tess stares at me, "You are so in denial," she rolls her eyes, and starts out the door.

I laugh softly, "Shut up," I say, not looking up from my phone. I keep typing.

Me: *I'm grateful to be your friend too <3*
See you in a few days

We make our way to the kitchen, where my parents and grandpa are preparing all of the delicious foods I've waited months to eat. Turkey with gravy, especially. Tess helps my grandpa set the table, and I bring out some of the sides. No sight of Jason. He never cared for Thanksgiving, but he would always eat the food and disappear into his room for the rest of the night to game with his friends.

I watch as my dad carves the turkey. "I set the dark meat aside just for you, buggy," he says, smiling. His dad joke apron we got him for Father's Day, is tied around his back.

I give him a quick hug. "Thanks, Dad."

We all sit around the table, and Jason finally appears in

sweats. Guess he couldn't even put on a pair of jeans for the occasion. He looks at me, but I don't look at him. I focus on getting the perfect scoop of mashed potatoes and stuffing. I top it with a hefty pour of gravy. Of course, he sits right on the other side of me. We've had the same spots since we were little. We never wanted to be separated.

Everything is delicious as always. I help my parents with the dishes, and Tess wipes down the table. I can tell she would rather be with her own family, but mine really likes her, so I hope she's okay.

"I'm going to go call my parents and brother if that's okay?" she asks, setting the towel on the table.

I smile, "For sure, I'll be on the patio swing when you're done."

She nods and goes off to my room. The dishes are done, so I grab my book and head to the swing. I brush some of the leaves off and sit on it with my legs crossed. I'm not even two pages in before I hear the door open. I look up, and Jason comes out of the house.

I can feel him moving toward me. "Can we talk now?"

I don't look at him. "No, I'm reading."

"Sades, please," he pleads.

I slam my book shut. "Don't call me that," I say sharply. I stand up and I start down the porch stairs.

"Sadie, stop."

"I'm going on a walk," I say, setting my book on the railing.

"Why do you have these walls up all of a sudden?" he says.

I stop dead in my tracks at the end of the driveway. I turn to face him, still on the porch.

I yell at him, "You mean the walls that you built?" I point my finger at him. I start to backpedal again.

"Sadie," he says, stepping down from the porch. "Wait."

I start to run "Go away." I look away from him.

"Sadie, I wish I had stopped him."

I stop again in front of the yard and close my eyes. Those words hit hard in my chest. I knew it. At least he finally brings it up.

"But that's the thing," I point my finger at him again, "You *could've* and you *chose* not to." Tears start streaming down my face and into my mouth. "Now I'm stuck with all this trauma and PTSD," I breathe as deeply as I can. "I got shipped away from the only home I have ever known to fight to make sense of myself after he ripped everything away from me, Jason." I finish. My face is still drenched with tears, but I quickly wipe them away. Snot runs down my nose. "And you're partially to blame for it," I finish.

Now he's standing in front of me in the middle of the street. "So don't tell me I have walls up," my voice shaking. He stammers, looking for something he can say to make it better. But he can't. Nothing he could say can undo the damage Chase did. As much as he likes to try.

I watch a tear fall from his eye. "I'm sorry, Sadie," he says, looking at me.

"Leave me alone," I finish and walk away again. I thought he might follow me, but he doesn't.

He wouldn't.

I walk through my neighborhood and the ones surrounding ours. Searching for some clarity in my old life. Clarity, I will probably never find. I don't feel at peace here anymore. I love my home, I always will. But nothing could ever erase what happened here. This place destroyed me. Ruined me. I can't rebuild myself in the same spot that tore me down. Surrounded by the people who watched it happen and pretended they didn't see.

* * *

Tess is lying on my bed when I come back from my walk. "Are you okay?" she asks as soon as I open the door.

I flop onto my bed next to her. "How do you know what happened?"

"I went to the bathroom while Jason was talking to your mom in the living room and overheard," she says, putting her laptop away.

I nod and stare at the ceiling. "What did my mom say?"

"She just said that you'll come around eventually."

I nod slowly, "Eventually," I say in frustration.

She gives me a look, "He's your brother," she adds.

"Yeah, and he screwed it up," I say. "Bad."

"I don't disagree," she starts, "family is family," she replies.

I nod and watch my ceiling fan go round and round. She's right, he's still my brother. But it's going to take a lot to rebuild what he broke. It's not easy to move on. But maybe I need to try. To really put it all in the past.

25

~tilting

A couple of days after we returned from Thanksgiving, things were… weird. Weird, as in I've thought a lot about what Julia and Tess said about things blowing up in my face. Things are just weird in general. Especially being back in that place. That spot. I still haven't talked to Jason, but I feel a lot better getting my feelings off my chest and into the open.

"Okay, everyone, today is going to look a little different," Clara says. We're in the big room like we were instructed to be yesterday. I look at Tess next to me and raise an eyebrow. We don't really do much besides work on our murals.

Christmas isn't far away. These three weeks between Thanksgiving and Christmas always drag for me.

"We're doing a splatter project," she continues.

"Oh boy," I hear Derek under his breath. We were told to wear crappy clothes, so I guess we should've expected this.

"It's time to let loose," she finishes with a smile. I'm scared of what we're about to endure. She motions for all of us to follow her out of the room, but to leave our things. My phone is buzzing. It's Julia calling. I just saw her, so I'll call her when we're done. I slip my phone in my bag and run to catch up with the rest of them. Levi smiles at me. He told me he liked my outfit, even though it's a ratty old shirt and shorts.

We walk into a room down the hall, and it's lined with plastic on the walls and floor. In the center, there are a million jars of different colored paints and brushes galore. All four of us look at each other and shrug. That's the thing about being here. We've all adapted to trying new things and not being afraid of being messy. That's good for people like us.

"There are no rules," Clara announces, "just let loose and have some fun," she says proudly, leaving the room. I nod slowly and go to the center and grab a brush. No one else moves but me. I scoop up a ton of blue paint and turn to face Derek.

"Don't do it, Sades," he says, holding his hand up.

I smirked at him, "I know your favorite color is blue, Derek," I taunt with an evil smile before whipping the paint on his face. More than once. Tess covers her mouth and laughs before grabbing a brush of her own.

She dips it in the brown, "and I know brown is yours," she sings, staring at me and smiling before absolutely annihilating me with the brown paint. My mouth drops as the brown paint drips down the front of my chest.

"It's on," I say with a straight face. After that, it is just a madhouse. Levi picks me up and lays me on the ground before taking green and dripping it all over my body from above.

"LEVI," I yell at him, covering my face. He laughs, and before I know it, Derek is hovering over me too. This time with purple paint. He joins Levi in the fun of dripping paint all over me. They know better than to get it in my hair, though. For the first time in a while, I forgot about everything. Everything from home, everything from here, that's so complicated. We're just allowed to *let loose*. I've been dreaming of feeling this way. To feel free and light.

I sit in the corner watching everyone throw paint at each other. For a room full of damaged kids, there are a lot of smiling faces. *I love it.* I catch a glimpse of Levi coming toward me out of the corner of my eye. He has his hand behind his back, and he's looking directly at me with a sneaky face. He starts throwing paint at me over and over again. He came with 3 separate brushes behind his back. I laugh as he grabs me and picks me up. He spins me around as he dumps paint down my back. He sets me down but doesn't move his hands. We just stare at each other. We move our eyes after a while when Tess starts throwing more at us both. I look like a rainbow of colors. Covered in paint. Clara did reassure us that it's washable, so I'm not worried about that. I just think about how lucky I am to experience this. I'm grateful for this place and these people. They're all I need. My past is in my past, and I'm no longer that girl. He's no longer a part of me.

We take towels to wipe off all the paint we can, and Clara tells us we didn't have to paint today if we didn't want to, but Derek and I agreed to come back later after we shower and change to work for a little bit. It's almost done. And I'm proud of it. Our vision really came to life. I wait for the rest of them to finish cleaning themselves up before we can head out. Maybe this is what healing looks like. Messy. Unpredictable. Beautiful.

We run to grab our things from the other room. I grab my things as I talk to Tess. The four of us start to walk out of the building. We're laughing and joking about how dumb we look. I grab my phone out of my bag once we get outside and flip it over. The screen lights up with at least 25 missed calls from Julia and my parents, and what seems like a million texts. I cock my head, confused.

"Hello there, Sadie," a harsh voice says. I glance up from my phone and see *him* standing there. I stop in my tracks in disbelief. I step backwards and almost fall.

"Who is that Sades?" Derek says loudly, looking from me to him. My mouth opens, but nothing comes out. My breath quickens, but I can't look away from him.

"Yeah, *Sades,*" he says, getting closer with his devilish smile.

I was reading my book on his beanbag in his room. I had tried to leave, but he didn't let me. Wanted me to stay until he was done playing his game.

"I'm done now," he said, walking toward me. I nodded and kept reading. "I said I'm done." His voice was harsh and loud. He towered over me. I didn't look up. The next thing I knew, his hand met my face. My jaw dropped, and he grabbed my wrist and pulled me off the bean bag. "Are you deaf?" he finished. He threw me on his bed. He hit me once more.

"Chase, come here quick," his mom yelled from upstairs.

"Don't move," he said as he pointed at me. I stayed there in terror. I didn't move. Not yet. My phone was still in my pocket. My bag was still near the door. I sobbed quietly. Horrified. I got up quietly and slipped my shoes on before I slipped out his side door.

I dialed Jason's number, but no answer. I tried again. No answer. As soon as I was out of sight of the house, I made a run for it. I heard the door open and slam shut.

"SADIE, COME BACK NOW!"

Everything around me blurs, and the night comes back in full horror.

I hear him continue to yell. I don't look back. My feet heavily scrape the pavement as I move my legs faster than I ever have before. I have to. A horn blares as I cross the street, not recognizing where I am. I turn wide-eyed, hoping I lost him. I didn't. He's close behind. I can feel his breath as he tries to take mine. His rough hands take hold of the back of my neck. My mouth is wide, but nothing is escaping from it. Fists clenched, I open my eyes to see the sky. The ground slips out from underneath me. As my head strikes the pavement, darkness envelopes me, swallowing me whole.

I blink. My heart pounds inside my chest. Tess moves beside me. Levi steps in front of me slightly.

"Step back, man," Derek says, sharp this time.

But Chase doesn't.

"You really thought I wouldn't find you, babe?" he says, getting closer and closer. "That restraining order was really bold of you," he finishes. I close my eyes, hoping this is all a dream. A nightmare that I need to wake up from. Except when I open my eyes, he's even closer to me. We're breathing the same air.

Derek glances back and forth between us. My breath quickens. My chest tightens. I can feel my pulse in my throat.

His shoes scrape against the pavement.

A single step closer.

I turn and *bolt.*

26

~fading into light

I run all the way back to the apartment without stopping. I don't look back. But I don't hear footsteps running after me. Just a lot of yelling. I take the stairs, there's no time to wait for the elevator. I sprint inside my room and lock the door. I shove two of my chairs in front of the door, along with my shoe rack. I fall onto the floor. Collapsed in a puddle of my own tears. My bag lies next to me, and my phone is continually buzzing. I don't answer. I can't move. My heart is pounding into another dimension. My breathing quickens, and I sit up to catch my breath.

I can't.

I grab onto the chair to brace myself. I'm lost. I don't know what to do. Or how he found me. Is that what all the missed calls were about earlier?

My breathing finally slows, and I stand up and walk to my balcony. I carefully peek out from behind my curtains to see three cop cars in front of the art building. My breathing quickens again. I watch as two police officers snap handcuffs onto him while he's face down on the ground. I cover my mouth with my hand and continue to sob. I couldn't watch them load him into the car.

I go into my room and shut the door. Still covered in paint and my makeup completely ruined, I get in the shower with all my clothes on. I sit on the floor of the shower for what feels like hours. I don't move. Just let the paint wash off and run down the drain. I watch it circle the drain before it disappears. Eventually, the water turns cold, and I force myself into dry clothes. Leaving the wet ones on the floor, I crawl into my bed.

* * *

I lay in my bed for hours. I don't move. I don't check my phone. I don't close my eyes. The ceiling fan is circling above my head. Slow and taunting me. My body feels heavy, like I've become one with the mattress. I keep replaying everything. His haunting voice, the way he smiled, like I still belonged to him. The way I ran like my life depended on it again. I should feel safe now. But I don't.

It's horrifying how quickly the past can crawl out of the shadows and sneak up on you. I thought I had buried it. Moved on. And then it showed up right in front of me, wearing the same face and calling me the same name.

I just want to disappear. How do I explain this to them? I'm sweating, but I pull another blanket on top of me. My weighted blanket. Does this ever really end? Or do I just have to carry it for the rest of my life?

As my head struck the pavement that day, I woke up to the sound of beeping and the smell of bleach stung my nose. My throat was dry. My body ached. Something tugged at the inside of my arm.

I tried to sit up and take deep breaths. Not remembering everything that happened. My arm was in a blue sling, and I touched my face and felt the cuts on my lip. I had moved the blanket to reveal the purple and yellow bruises all over my legs. A sharp pain had cut through my skull. My parents were asleep on the couch across the room, and the darkness from outside crept into the white, stale room.

I had made it out.

I had made it out.

But at what cost?

* * *

My phone is still on the floor somewhere. I haven't picked it up since yesterday. It's probably dead. My alarm clock reads 11:00 am. The sun is peeking through my window, so it woke me up. Otherwise, I would've kept sleeping all day.

There's a gentle knock on my door. It startles me at first. I don't get up. Whoever it is keeps knocking, but it's soft. *It's Derek.* I can tell by his knock.

"No one's home," I yell at the door. He doesn't respond, he just keeps knocking. "Seriously, go away," I yell again, pulling the blanket over my head. He keeps knocking. He won't stop until I open the door, so I crawl out of bed and move the chairs from in front of the door back to their original spot. Same with the shoe rack. I have mascara dried all over my face, and my hair is up in a messy bun. I take a deep breath, preparing myself to face him. To face Derek after all of that.

I slowly open the door. "I want to be alo-" in my doorway is Julia. My tears start immediately as she rushes in to hug me. Between sobs, I look up and see Derek behind her. He smiles softly and walks away. Julia pulls away and shuts the door behind her.

"What are you doing here?" I ask, still crying slowly. I plop onto my couch and look at the ceiling.

"Derek called me," she sits next to me. She puts her hand on mine and holds it tight. "You weren't answering anyone's calls, and he was really worried," she finishes.

I nod, "I don't know where my phone is," I say, looking around the living room. She gets up and finds it on the floor in the kitchen.

"Here, you need to respond to your friends," she says, handing me the phone.

Derek had texted me a few times and called several times. I click on his name to respond to him first.

Me: *Thank you*

Next, I click on Tess's text. She also called and texted a million times.

Me: *im ok. Julia is here. I'll call you later*

She starts typing almost immediately.

Tess: *okay, I love you so much*

I heart her message and move on to my parents. I don't think they don't know much of what happened, so I just tell them that I'm okay. No text from Jason. I wonder if he knew he was coming out here to find me. Lastly, Levi.

Levi: *please call me when you get this.*

"I should call him, right?" I say, showing Julia the text.

"No, just text him and say you'll call him later," she says. She's probably right.

Me: *im fine ill call u later*

"I can't believe he showed up here," I say, throwing my pillow at the wall. "I finally thought he was in the past," I pace around my living room. Julia just watches me. There's something about her company that's so comforting. I feel a little at peace.

"I called you so many times yesterday because Jason told me Chase had put something on his story about coming to New Haven, so he assumed he was coming to find you."

"Jason called you?" I say, still pacing.

"Mhm," she replies. I nod and bite my fingernails.

"You may not want to see this, but someone recorded the whole thing and posted it," she says, pulling out her phone.

"You're joking." I sit down next to her and stare at her phone. I'm not in the video, thank goodness. After I ran off, Chase tried to follow me. Derek cut him off. Chase swung but missed. Derek didn't even hesitate after that. One punch straight to his jaw knocked him to the ground. I just stare at the screen, stunned.

"No way," I say, getting closer to the phone. "Who called the cops?" I ask her.

"Derek told me Levi did," she says, pausing the video.

"Oh," I start, "hit play."

Chase is lying on the ground, and as he is about to get up, Derek puts his foot on his chest and pushes him back down, and holds him there. The video cuts off after the cops show up and start putting him in handcuffs. I pretended not to notice how attractive that was.

"I can't believe he did that," I murmur, lying back on the couch in disbelief.

"Are you okay, Sades?" she asks, pulling me in for another hug.

"Yeah, I'll be fine, I think," I start, "as long as he stays in jail," I continue.

"He better," she says, making a fake mad face.

"How long are you staying?" I ask, hoping she'd say all day.

"I have to work at 4:00, so I have to leave by 1:30," she says, grabbing my hands again. I nod and lie down. Julia and I watch a movie for a while before she has to go. I don't deserve her sometimes. She shows up for me without hesitation. I'll always need Julia. No matter where I am.

"Thanks for coming, Jules," I say, walking with her toward the door.

"I'd fly across the country if you needed me," she says, hugging me. "I love you, I'll see you in a few weeks for your mural display," she smiles. I nod and give her another hug. Julia has always given the best hugs. Even as kids, if I was mad or upset, all she had to do was hug me and I'd feel better. Even if I don't like hugs all that much, hers always make me feel calm.

I open the door for her to leave, and standing outside my door, about to knock, are Tess, Levi, and Derek. Tess with a tray of coffee cups and Levi carrying a grocery bag filled with goodies.

"You didn't think we'd leave you alone, did you?" Tess says, walking in like she owns the place. She hands me a warm cup. "Your usual."

Levi lifts the bag. "We got the essentials," he smiles at me. "Ice cream, cookies, your microwave popcorn, and a good old Christmas candle," he finishes, shoving the candle in my face so I can smell it.

"Yummy," I say, grabbing a lighter to light it.

"Love you, Jules," I say as she walks out the door.

"Love you more," she replies as everyone else waves bye to her. Levi throws a bag of popcorn into the microwave. I sit on the floor in front of my couch, and Tess sits directly behind me on the couch. I lay my head in between her legs. She runs her fingers through my knotted hair.

Derek sits on the ground next to me. "I saw the video," I say in a whisper so only he can hear me.

He makes a face, "Sorry you had to see that," he admits.

"I'm not," I say, grabbing his face with both my hands, "thank you, D."

He nods. "Not a chance that fool gets anywhere near you," he says, smiling and placing his hand softly under my chin. The microwave beeps, and Levi brings the popcorn over to me. I indulge in it. I hadn't eaten dinner last night or breakfast yet this morning. I also chug the latte from Tess.

The candle flickers, and the room is quiet. No one is forcing me to talk about how I feel. Just letting me be comfortable with them. Levi pulls a blanket off my couch and drapes it over me on the floor. I lay down on the ground, and they all join me on the floor. Levi is right in my eye line.

I close my eyes for a moment, and Levi nudges me. "Hey, we're here. You don't have to face any of this alone."

Tess smiles down at me, "Whenever you're ready, we'll help you get through it."

I wipe away my tears that come back and manage a small smile. "Love you guys," I say, sitting back up.

"We love you," Tess says, grabbing my hand. We sit in silence for a while. The weight of the world is on my shoulders.

But at least I know that where I am, I won't get hurt.

27

~off track

I move my brush back and forth across our canvas. I have a large mountain of gray paint we are using for the background. Nothing fancy, just gray. We really want to highlight the tree, and nothing else can distract from it.

My friends are tiptoeing around me, I can tell. I wish I could just tell them to act normally and that everything will go back to how it was. But it's not normal. Normal isn't your abusive ex showing up to do who knows what. Normal isn't wondering if he'll stay in jail. Normal isn't being afraid he might show up again. Maybe normal is dumb. Maybe it's okay to not be normal. I've accepted that, I think.

I get up on the step stool to get the gray on the very top of the painting, but I can't quite reach it. "Can you help me?" I ask Derek timidly.

He gets up from his stool, "Yes, I can," he grabs my brush from my hand, and we trade spots. He helps me down from the stool by grabbing my hand and resting his hand on my back. He gets up on the stool and paints above the tree. Being extra careful not to paint onto the tree accidentally. I just watch him.

"You doing okay?" he asks, looking down at me from the stool.

"Yeah, yeah, I'm good," I say, without making eye contact. "How's your hand?" I ask. I replay in my mind how hard he hit him. How it immediately sent him to the ground.

He looks down at his other hand and stretches out his fingers. "Doctor said it's not broken, just bruised, so all good," he says, smiling at me. He would do it again if he had to. I know he would.

"That's good." We don't talk while he finishes the spot I couldn't reach. I'm so focused on watching him paint.

"Guys," Tess startles me, and she pushes her way into our art room.

I jump slightly and spill some paint on my leg. "Geez, why you gotta sneak up on us like that?" I reply, turning toward her standing in the doorway.

"Shoot, sorry," she says, sitting on one of our stools.

Derek finally turns around, "What's up?"

She places her hands on the table and gives us one of her devious smirks like she's up to something. "Levi just told me his uncle owns a ski resort in New York," she smiles big.

She pauses. Derek and I look at each other and back at her. "And?"

"Anddd we're going this weekend," she claps her hands a few times.

My head falls into my hands, "I can't ski," I say, looking at her.

"I can teach you," Derek chimes in.

Tess throws her hands up, "he'll teach you!" She winks at me.

I let out a sigh, "Ughhh, why do you guys make me do things every weekend?" I whine.

Tess grabs my hands, "because it's good for all of us," she smiles.

I nod and grab my pallet. She isn't wrong, and I could definitely use a distraction right now. But does it really have to be skiing? The last time I even stepped foot near a hill of snow was when we went sledding on a hill behind our house, like 3 years ago. One of our old friends from high school made a jump, and I flew off of it and broke my wrist. So not a huge fan of snowy, icy hills. But it's worth another try, I think.

* * *

Levi is the last to join us, waiting in the lobby. "Does everyone have snow pants and a jacket?" he asks, adjusting his backpack on his back. We all nod and grab our stuff off the ground. We load it all into Levi's pickup, and Tess and I hop in the back seat. We have gotten some snow, but not a lot. I guess I wasn't aware that ski resorts can make fake snow.

"I'm so excited to drink hot chocolate and sit in the lodge," Tess says, clapping her hands.

"You are going to ski, though, right?" Derek asks, turning around from the front seat.

"Probably," she says and smiles.

I laugh and look out the window while we get on the highway. "Are we all sharing a room?" I ask quietly.

Levi makes eye contact with me through the rear-view mirror, "No, I got us two rooms," he says, and looks back at the road.

"Oh, okay," I say, trying not to sound disappointed. Some time with Tess would be nice, though. I liked hanging out with her during Thanksgiving.

The drive isn't long, maybe close to two hours or so. We drive through New York City, which brings me back to when Derek and I were there. I open Instagram and find the selfie we took in Times Square. Things were simpler then. When our feelings weren't so complicated and I wasn't always feeling conflicted about everything. I think about the steak we had at that one steakhouse by Broadway. It was so good, and Derek made fun of me for getting mine medium well. Told me it ruins the whole steak. But it made me laugh when the steak came out, and I needed steak sauce because it was so dry. He never let me live it down. I had tried his medium-rare steak and actually enjoyed it. Safe to say I'll never go back to eating medium-well steak drenched in steak sauce.

Levi turns onto a long, windy road. It's buried beneath tall trees covered in snow. The resort finally comes into view.

"This place looks sick," Derek says, looking out his window. He looks back at me and smiles, "Can't wait to show you the ropes," he winks. I smile, and Tess gives me a look. I shrug and make a face like I don't know what he's doing. Tess is never oblivious. She is always paying attention to people's facial cues and body language. She can catch onto anything. Nothing gets by Tess O'Brien.

We lug our suitcases up to our rooms. Tess and I open our door, and it's a literal suite. "I can't believe his uncle hooked us up with this," I say, opening the curtains to reveal the beautiful view of the mountains.

"Yeah, this is crazy, I've never been in a place this nice before," she says, getting her snow stuff out.

"We're going skiing already?" I complain.

"Uh, yeah, we only have two days here," she says, braiding her long black hair and putting a beanie over it.

"Can you do my hair?"

She nods and pats the chair for me to sit on.

"Sadie, I've never been more confused about someone's love life than I am with yours." She laughs, and I can see her face in the mirror.

I roll my eyes and laugh awkwardly, "What's there to be confused about?"

"Which one are you dating, because to an outsider it's not very clear," she ties an elastic around the bottom of my braid.

"Neither."

"You have two guys fawning over you, and you're acting like you don't notice," she starts. "At least you have people interested in you." Her voice trails off.

"Um, what about Josh?" I ask, "Your boyfriend?"

She hesitates, "We broke up a couple of nights ago."

I whip around to face her, "What?!" I stare at her, "Why didn't you say anything?"

"Because it's not a big deal," she says.

"Tess," I look at her.

"What? I honestly just realized after being here for a while that he wasn't what I needed anymore," she pauses, "and that's okay with me."

"I'm sorry," I start, but she cuts me off.

"Stop, it's fine, I'm good," she resumes braiding my hair. "But for real, Sades, don't lead both of them on any longer, especially Levi," she finishes.

"What do you mean, especially Levi?" I ask, making eye contact with her in the mirror. She doesn't respond right away.

"Just follow your heart, especially if it says Derek, because that man has been yearning for you since we got here," she

175

says, putting her hand on her hip.

I roll my eyes. "I couldn't tell, so..."

"That's because you're blind," she taps my shoulders and spins me around in the chair. "Go get dressed, we have some slopes to shred," she smiles.

I hope she's okay. I know she has a hard time bringing up her problems, so she doesn't take up too much attention. She told me it comes from being in the shadow of her brother's medical issues. So we get it. But she knows we're here for her. And she'll open up when she wants to. I won't force her.

We meet the boys at the ski rental. Levi helps me find ones that fit me and helps me put them on. "You know how to get on and off the ski lift?" he asks, strapping my boots in.

I shake my head, "can't be that hard."

"You'd be surprised," Derek chimes in after getting his boots on. I've never seen him in a beanie before. His curls peak out from under it on his forehead.

"Should I be scared?" I laugh.

Derek shakes his head, "nah, we'll show you." he smiles and helps me up. We grab our helmets and head out of the lodge.

"I want to get a picture," I say, pulling my phone out of my pocket. I ask the lift operator and he complies. We get together in our huge snow gear that makes me feel like a marshmallow and smile. I don't even have to force it.

I stare at the lift and look at Derek.

"It's okay, you basically just stand there and let it take you, getting off is the more difficult part, but I'll tell you how to do that on the way up," he smiles, and we make our way toward the lift. I nod and stand in front of Tess and Levi, talking about what they want for dinner. I swear Levi is always talking about food.

I laugh to myself. "I'm going to fall," I look at Derek.

"Probably," he laughs.

I hit his arm, "Derek."

"It's okay to fall, though," he finishes.

"Yeah, okay, until I'm on my back and you guys laugh at me," I say, smiling at him.

"Fair," he says as it's almost our turn. He was right, you do just stand there, and it swoops you up.

We ride up, and Derek tells me how to get off, but something tells me it won't be as easy as he makes it sound.

Derek and I turn around to look at them behind us. Levi has a straight face, and Tess is messing with her helmet. I wave at Levi, but he just gives me this forced smile.

I turn back around. "Is Levi okay?" I ask Derek.

He looks back at him, too. "I assume so," he shrugs.

We're almost at the top. I know how to use my skis already. I practiced before, but never got on a hill. Hopefully, Derek can help me so I don't eat it coming down.

We get off the lift, and I almost fall, but I keep my balance. It's the bunny hill, so I'm not scared.

"Ready?" Derek looks at me as the other two get off the lift.

"Born ready," I say in my cheesy movie voice. Levi shows off by going ahead of us and doing some sort of trick going down the hill before he disappears. I start down the hill slowly, just trying to keep my balance.

Derek laughs and guides me down, "Here, hold onto my arm till you can get the hang of it," he says, holding his arm out. I grab on.

Eventually, I get the hang of it. "I think I got it!" I turn to him, going down the hill faster now. I let go of his arm and do it on my own. Tess is just ahead of us. She's also very good at skiing, so she turns around and snaps a picture of Derek and me. I hold up a peace sign and he copies me. I start to pick up speed and laugh as I go down the rest of the hill. I've been craving this kind of adrenaline.

Once at the bottom, I don't think anything could erase the smile plastered across my face. "Again," I say. I'm the last one down, but everyone waited for me.

"Tougher hill this time?" Levi asks.

I cock my head to the left, "uh, no," I laugh.

And we go again. And again. And again. Each time, I get better and can keep up with the rest of them. But wow, is it exhausting!

We went back to the lodge. But it's not quite time to eat, so we decide to find a hot tub. I love hot tubs. They're so relaxing. We used to have one at our house in Vermont, but my dad eventually sold it when we moved out. I miss that hot tub dearly.

28

~white noise

Back in our room, Tess and I change into bikinis and grab the robes from the closet. We take mirror selfies in our fancy robes and grab something to drink on our way down. They're already in the hot tub when we get there. Tess immediately takes off her robe and gets in. I watch Levi watch her get in. Not exactly in adoration, but let's be honest, who wouldn't look at Tess?

I don't take off my robe yet and just sit on the edge and dip my feet in. Need to acclimate to the water first.

"Just get in," Tess says, looking up at me.

"Fine," I grab my claw clip off the table and throw my hair up in it. Levi is on the phone with his uncle in the hot tub. Hopefully, he doesn't drop his phone in.

Nervously, I take off my robe and throw it behind me. I watch as Derek watches me do so. He clears his throat and grabs his drink off the edge. My blue bikini shows my tan stomach. "This is so nice," I say softly, lowering myself in.

"What are we gonna do for dinner?" Tess asks.

Levi hangs up his phone and puts it away from the water.

"There's a pizza place we could go pick up?"

"Yes, perfect," Tess says. She turns the bubbles on, and they flood the hot tub. I close my eyes and tilt my head back to just enjoy the warmth.

"So what did you think of skiing Sades?" Derek asks me.

I open my eyes and look at him. "I really liked it," I smile.

We all go quiet again. Derek gets up to go to the bathroom, but I don't know how it wasn't freezing when he got out. I slide over toward Levi, "hi," I say, looking at him. Tess pretends not to watch us.

He puts his fingers on my shoulder, and I feel the water drip off of them. "Hi."

I look at his eyes and down at his chest. "Can we get sausage on the pizza?" I ask him.

He nods, "Of course, we can," he pauses, "Speaking of which, I should order," he grabs his phone. He calls the restaurant and places our order. One pepperoni and one sausage. "It'll be ready in twenty. Tess, want to come with me to get it?" he turns toward her. She nods.

I scoot away from him. Trying to hide the disgusted look on my face. Why wouldn't he ask me? Tess and I lock eyes, and she shrugs slightly. Is he avoiding me? Derek comes back and hands me another drink. "Thanks," I say, trying not to sound annoyed. Because I am.

We all decide to get out and come back after dinner. I pull Levi aside before they leave. Derek and Tess walk away. I wrap a towel around myself to dry off before putting my robe back on. "Why didn't you ask me to come with you?" I ask. My annoyed tone is coming out now.

He shrugs and looks away, "figured you'd want to stay here," he says, not looking at me.

I nod, "Got it."

"Will you get drinks and stuff? We'll meet you guys back in my room," he says.

I nod again, "sure." I roll my eyes slightly, but he doesn't see.

"Perfect," he says, kissing my forehead. It catches me off guard. I turn to walk away and see Derek watching us. As soon as we make eye contact, he looks away and starts to walk inside.

They leave to get the pizza, and Derek and I put our robes back on over our swimsuits so we could come back later. "Want to go check out the rest of the lobby?" I ask him. He just nods, and we start walking around the back of the resort, where there are restaurants and a bowling alley. This place is so fancy, and we definitely look out of place.

All of a sudden, Derek's vibe changes. He was not acting like he was earlier on the hill. I hate when he does this. "What's wrong?" I pry.

He shrugs, "nothing."

I look at him, "Derek."

He looks away from me and tucks his hands in his pocket. "You and Levi still talking?" he asks.

I wasn't expecting that. "Yeah, I guess so," I shrug.

We keep walking, and he doesn't say anything else right away. "He's not right for you, Sadie," he says harshly, stopping in his tracks. We're by the main parking lot and the entrance. There are a lot of people wandering around.

I look around nervously at all the people. "What?" I say, stopping too. He doesn't respond. Just looks everywhere but at me.

He inches closer to me, "he's just not," he mumbles. Almost under his breath.

"Why do you get to decide what's right for me?"

He finally makes eye contact. My stomach churns. "I guess I don't," he says uncomfortably. He turns and starts to walk away.

I grab his arm and pull him back. "Derek, I don't understand why this bothers you so much," I mumble. Except I might know. But I'm hoping he won't say it.

He takes a deep breath before speaking. My gut tightens. "I heard you that one night, talking to Julia," he pauses. I rack my brain for what he could be talking about. "When we first got here. You told her you didn't want a relationship while you were here," he looks at me with hurt in his eyes. "And you know I respected that because I knew you were hurt and needed a friend. So that's what I was, a good friend."

"Derek I-I" I stammer softly. Having no idea what to say. I didn't even know that he heard that conversation.

He interrupts me, "But really it's not that you didn't want a relationship." he pauses, glancing up and locking eyes with me. "You just didn't want one with me," his voice cracks. My heart sinks. My mouth is open, but no words escape from it. This is the most honest I've ever seen him. It kills me. I stare at him. His eyes are heavy.

I can't even argue with him. That it wasn't about him. That I wasn't ready. But that all sounds like a load of crap now, doesn't it? Because I let someone in even when I swore I wouldn't.

Levi.

And maybe it does look like I just didn't want Derek. But it's not true.

It's not fair.

He looks away and takes a deep breath. "You have no idea what it's like to fall for you, Sadie," he says, looking back at me. I flinch when he says that. Tears start to crawl down his face. My mouth is still open, fishing for words to say. "And to have to watch you fall for someone else," he finishes wiping the tears from his face. I just stand there. Trying to figure out what I'm supposed to say. I need to say something, anything. I never thought he would admit that. But part of me doesn't believe it. Believe him. Believe that anyone would love me again.

I inhale, but my breath gets caught. "I-I didn't know you felt that way," I stammer.

He shrugs, "How would you?" he tucks his hands in his pockets. I can see the hurt on his face. The betrayal. But he doesn't have the right to be mad that I didn't know. That I couldn't see it even when everyone else could.

My lungs fill with the cold air, "Maybe because you told Levi that New York didn't mean anything." I reply coldly. I never thought I'd bring that up.

He pinches the bridge of his nose and exhales slowly. "Sadie, I didn't mean that, *you know* I didn't."

"No, Derek, I didn't," I shout, but then lower my voice. I grab both sides of my head and yank on my hair. "How was I supposed to know that?"

"I-I don't know, Sadie. I'm sorry."

I don't say anything else. Because what am I supposed to say? Why would he say that if he didn't mean it?

He gulps, his adam's apple rising then falling quickly. "Of course, New York meant something," he stammers.

I shake my head slowly, "You don't get to say that now." I pause as my hair whips in my face from the wind. "Not after you made me feel like I was imagining it all." I throw my hands into the air and break our eye contact.

"You weren't imagining it," he says, getting closer to me. He grabs my hand as the collar of his shirt picks up in the wind. My tears have dried, but his haven't. He looks at me with eyes full of regret.

I want to believe him. Gosh, I want to. "Then why didn't you fight for me?"

He hesitates, "Because I was scared." he admits.

"Scared of what?" I ask harshly, pulling my hands away from his and placing them on my hips.

He backs up and starts to pace back and forth. "Of losing you when I just got you." A heavy silence falls over us. The twinkle lights flicker above us. "My best friend," he starts, "I didn't want to ruin what we had."

I graze my forehead with my fingers, pressing into my skull. "Derek-" I start to speak, but then look toward the building. "Oh no."

He raises an eyebrow and turns to where I'm looking. "Crap." he murmurs under his breath. Tess and Levi are standing right in the doorway with the pizza.

Perfect.

* * *

We eat in their room, and I'm careful not to spill on Derek's bed. Levi sits next to me but doesn't say much.

Why does it feel like I just lost both of them in one night? They're still here, but they aren't *here.*

We finish and decide to skip the hot tub. According to Levi, we shouldn't wear ourselves out before we go skiing again tomorrow. I don't feel like skiing anymore. I want to go home and lie in my bed and ignore everyone.

"I'm tired, I'm gonna head back to our room," I say, getting up. Tess gets up with me. I know it isn't late, but my chest feels heavy and I need to talk to Tess.

"Oh, okay, sure," Levi says, picking up the deck of cards we were using.

Derek gets up and follows me to the door before Tess comes. "You okay?" he asks out of what feels like obligation.

I nod, "mhm, just tired," I say, twisting the door handle. "Goodnight."

He holds the door as Tess walks out, too. "Night, Sadie," he replies. "Night Tess," he finishes. Once we're about halfway down the hallway, I turn back to look at their room. He's still standing there watching us walk away. As soon as I see him, he shuts the door.

* * *

We get back to our room, and I completely flop on the bed and punch the bed like I'm a toddler throwing a temper tantrum, "ughhh I hate everything!" I whine.

"Is this because of that loaded conversation with Derek?" Tess asks, getting under her blanket.

I turn toward her and nod. "How much did you hear?" I ask hesitantly, unsure if I want to know the answer.

"I don't know..." she pauses, "like all of it."

I groan and cover my face with a pillow. "You're joking."

"Nope, and I can also say that Levi did not take it well," she continues.

I rip the pillow off my face. "Of course he didn't. Derek just told me he is in love with me while I'm still with Levi, I think..."

She takes a quick breath. "This is crazy," she laughs to herself. "Not helping."

"I know, I know, sorry."

I get up to go to the bathroom. I come back out mid-brushing my teeth. Mouth full of toothpaste, "What the heck do I do?" I start, "Tell me what to do, Tess."

"All I can tell you is that Derek has wanted you since the beginning," she says as she plugs her phone in and turns off the lamp.

"It's not my fault he couldn't be truthful," I spit out my toothpaste and brush my hair.

"Well, you couldn't either," she replies. She's right. I'm starting to feel like a broken record. But that was before he actually told me he had feelings for me. I like Levi, but part of me is realizing that Derek might've been right. He doesn't really get me or see me. And that's not necessarily his fault.

"Sorry, I feel like this is all we talk about lately," I say, getting into bed.

She shrugs, "Eh, don't worry about it, keeps my life entertaining."

"I'm glad my complicated love life is entertaining," I laugh. I shut the lights off and plug in my phone.

"Be honest now, then, Sadie." She whispers through the darkness.

I turn to face her even though I can't see her. "I wish I could."

"You'll get there, now that it's all out in the open," she whispers back.

I nod, and my hair rubs against the pillow, "love you."

"Love you always," she starts, "even though you have two boyfriends." She stifles a giggle.

I throw my extra pillow at her, but miss her completely.

"Good freaking night," I say while laughing too.

I watch as the snow falls outside our window. Lit up by the street lights. I've always loved the snow. I find it calming and peaceful. Even when it's blowing around and I have to shovel it off my car while my fingers freeze. It brings me some serenity. Which is exactly what I need right now.

* * *

We get ready to go skiing he next morning. Tess and I grab coffee from downstairs beforehand and a little breakfast. The boys eventually join us, but apparently, they want to go on the bigger, more dangerous hills today since we only did the bunny hills yesterday. It makes me feel bad, like I was wasting their time yesterday. I'm surprised they want to hang out together after what Derek said within earshot of Levi yesterday. Typically, I would be expecting some sort of fight, but none of that. Just two bros hanging out, I guess. I doubt they even acknowledged what he said or anything about me.

Tess and I bounce between the small hills and the lodge to warm up by the fire. We play games and listen to some good music. She became the friend I was scared to make when I came here, and I am so lucky.

* * *

When it starts to get dark, we decide to head back to New Haven a day early. We didn't really want to ski anymore, and it's not like we were paying for it. It's dark on the ride back. No one really talks. The soft indie music is playing on the radio in the background of our thoughts.

I told myself this trip would be fun. That it would be a distraction. But the truth is, I brought all of it with me. Every feeling I didn't want to deal with, every conversation I've been avoiding. Now it's hanging over my head, knowing I can't avoid it all much longer without hurting them.

I look up at Derek. His head against the headrest. I can't tell if he's sleeping or just sitting there in silence. The only time he has moved is to drink out of his water bottle.

The silence stretches, and my mind races for clarification. But what if I never find it?

29

~corruption

We got back around 8:00 pm, and since then, I haven't spoken to either of them. It's late now, almost midnight. The town of New Haven is still. I lie in bed staring at my ceiling, wondering what the absolute heck I'm going to do. I've never been one of those girls who can talk to multiple guys. I won't be that girl. I have to be honest with myself. Just like Julia and Tess said. So, I grab my phone off my nightstand.

Me: *You up?*

He replies almost instantly.

Levi: *Yeah, why?*

Me: *Meet me downstairs*

I throw on a sweatshirt over my tank top and head down in my outside slippers. The building smells like the crisp winter air. He's waiting in the lobby for me. Gray sweat pants and a flannel hoodie.

He looks up when I walk down. His soft smile is one I could recognize anywhere.

"Hey," I say quietly, approaching him. He doesn't say

anything at first. He exhales and walks toward me. "Want to take a walk?" I ask, motioning toward the door.

He nods and holds the door open for me.

I have no idea how to start this conversation. Before I can say something I may not mean wholeheartedly, he starts. "Sadie," he says calmly, "I can't do this."

I look at him, "Do what?"

He takes a deep breath and looks over at me as we walk down Main Street. "Be with you, knowing my friend is in love with you."

I don't say anything.

He continues, "I've seen the way Derek looks at you, Sadie." He breathes deeply and slows his walk. "You're all he's ever wanted."

"Levi," I start. But he interrupts me.

"I heard what he said outside the resort," he replies calmly.

"I know you did, and I'm sorry," I start, "I know I need to be honest."

"Okay, then be honest."

"I don't know what I want," I admit.

He doesn't respond, just looks down at his shoes, waiting for me to say more.

"But I know that being with you and being uncertain isn't fair to you," I say.

He looks up, finally, "You should be with the person you really want, Harper."

I stop and turn to him, "I'm sorry," I say.

He grabs my hands, "I'm not, you deserve to be happy," he says. "We're still friends," he continues, "and I'll always be in your corner."

I nod as tears start to fall from my eyes.

"It's okay," he says gently and wraps me up in a hug. "We promised each other that we would put ourselves first," he says.

"I know," I say.

"And if I'm being honest, too, I'm not sure a relationship is what I need right now," he says, pulling away.

"I'm sorry, Levi."

"I don't think it ever was, but I liked you, so I ignored other feelings I was having," he says.

"I really did like you too," I say, knowing it wouldn't make up for the fact that I *had* led him on for so long. We walk back in silence. But not so much an awkward silence. Because there wasn't anything left unsaid. At least not on my end.

We walk back into our building, and I look over at him. "Don't say anything to Derek yet, though. I need to talk to him first, if that's okay?"

He nods, "I get it."

He walks me to my room, and we stand outside my door. "See you tomorrow?" he asks.

I nod and begin to open my door.

"Make sure you take care of him, alright?" he says, holding the door open for me. I look at him, confused.

I nod, "I will," I say, even though I know Derek can handle himself and that he's doing well.

"Goodnight," he smiles and gives me a quick kiss on the cheek. I don't feel anything.

"Night," I say, closing the door behind me.

I climb back in bed and pull up my texts with Derek. I want to say something. Anything. But the time isn't right. I need to just wait. Just because Levi and I are over doesn't mean telling Derek is the right thing.

191

It may never be.

Because what if I tell him, and he's already starting to move on? Forgotten how he felt. What if I missed my chance, being too wrapped up in myself that I ignored everything that was right in front of me?

I stare at his name on the screen, my thumb hovering over the keyboard. I want to say something.

Hey, I dumped Levi for you.

Hey, I fell for you, too.

Hey, I've always wanted to be with you.

But I can't. I lock my phone and set it back on the nightstand. Maybe tomorrow I'll know what to do. But I doubt it. Making decisions is clearly not my thing. I close my eyes and try to forget it all.

I hope I didn't wait too long.

30

~slowly drying

"I heard you finally talked to Levi," Tess says as she approaches me at my spot.

I close my book, "Yeah, we had a good, honest conversation."

She nods and sits next to me. "That's good," she pauses. "It's not going to be weird though, right?"

I shake my head and smile, "We both knew we were better as friends." I hesitate. "No weirdness over here."

She nods slowly and looks around.

"I know what you're dying to ask, so just ask," I say, smiling.

She lets out a breath, "Okay, fine. Did you tell Derek?" she sits up straight, smiles, and raises her eyebrows.

I shake my head again. "I don't know how to, so I'm waiting." I sigh and pack up my stuff. "Come with me as a buffer in case it's awkward?" I plea, sticking my bottom lip out.

She nods and pulls me up off my seat.

I'm sure he doesn't know about Levi and me yet. If he did, that would make it feel more real, and I'm not sure if I'm ready for it to feel real yet. She comes down with me per my request, and after some small talk, she leaves to meet Levi.

I try to make myself seem as small as I can in our room. "Hey, can we talk?" I ask Derek. I don't know why I asked that. I haven't decided what I want to say to him yet.

"Can we later? I'm feeling the stress of this painting," he says with a soft laugh that lightens my mood.

I nod, "yeah, sure," I say, grabbing my paints.

It's Monday, meaning this is our last week. That's all the time we have left to finish this tree. The gallery is on Saturday night.

It's starting to feel repetitive at this point. Starting to wish we had picked something cooler like Tess and Levi's ocean thing. But it is way too late to change our minds.

Don't get me wrong, I think it's good. But what meaning does it really have? On one hand, it looks plain, but on the other hand, it almost represents the roughness but also gentleness of Derek and I's *friendship* since we got here. What used to be uncomplicated is now the most complicated thing in my life.

Not only did we show up to paint at like 10 am, but we're planning on being here till late tonight. We may have accidentally ditched a few too many sessions to go off and do whatever. But now we have a lot of work to catch up on if we want a shot at this scholarship.

I keep replaying the way Levi looked at me when he said goodnight. The way he stepped back and let me go. That hurt worse somehow. He didn't fight for me.

* * *

We spend all day painting, hardly taking breaks, and I fight the urge to say something. He doesn't act too differently, but obviously, he feels a little awkward. He did just spill his heart out to me after all. There are so many opportunities in our conversations where I could slip it in. Tell him what I want him to know. But I can't. Because jumping into something with Derek would make Levi right. Even though we both know he is, admitting that is extremely difficult. I don't want to hurt him any more than I already have.

The guilt builds in my chest and won't go away. I try to ignore it and focus on our tree. But it's almost impossible to ignore. Weighing my body down like a heavy snowfall on tree branches.

It's almost 3:00 now. I take a deep breath and sit back on my stool.

"Can we take a little break? I need to find a dress for the gallery, "I say to him.

He turns toward me with his paintbrush. "Yeah, sure," he agrees, "but I think I'll stay and keep working."

I put my hand on his shoulder to get up. I watch his face as it turns from a smile into a straight face. "Okay, be back in a little bit," I say, gathering my things. "You okay?" I add before walking out the door.

"Yeah, I'm good, why?" he replies.

"Just checking," I say with a smile. I walk out the door and wait for Tess in the lobby.

"I am so exhausted," I say as we walk to my car. It's below freezing outside and cloudy.

"Me too, girl, we've been here for what feels like days," she says, getting into the passenger seat.

I shift the car into gear and head toward the mall. "Did Levi seem okay today?" I ask her

"Yeah, I think so?" The car goes silent. "So….did you tell Derek?" she says, smiling ear to ear.

I gently hit her arm, "You already asked that earlier," I say.

"You guys just spent hours alone together," she says, staring at me.

I groan, "I know, but I couldn't do it," I say.

"Are you going to tell him?" she asks, poking my arm.

"I don't know."

We pull into the mall parking lot, and it's not very busy. "Sadie, you have to. That man is in love with you," she says.

I shift the car into park. "It's not the right time," I say.

"Girl, be for real," she says, getting out of the car.

"Next topic," I say, walking in the mall, "let's make this quick, please."

She nods and goes into the first store she sees. I'm not going to be picky, but it's also freezing outside, so I need to be ready for any weather. I'm looking for a long-sleeve dress that's classy enough for our mural. Derek said he was going to wear his one brown suit, so I need to find something to match.

We look around a couple of stores, and I finally found one that isn't horrible. It's a tight, short, brown long-sleeve dress. It's simple, but I think it'll be good for the gallery. "I'm getting this one," I say, holding up the dress for Tess to see.

"Oh yes, Derek's jaw will drop when he sees you in that," she says, smirking at me.

"I'm gonna kill you," I say, walking to check out.

We walk back out to my car. It's snowing now. I think we're supposed to get a snowstorm this weekend, which is a little inconvenient for the gallery. I get in the car and slam the door shut against the wind.

She puts her shopping bags in the back seat. "Let's head back before they both freak out," she says.

"I think the stress is getting to Derek," I laugh softly, "because it's getting to me too." We both laugh.

"I'm chillin'," she says.

"I'm glad," I roll my eyes.

* * *

We rush inside, trying not to slip on the icy sidewalk, and shake the snow off our coats as we head down the hallway. Derek's still at it, focused, and looks like he's been working nonstop. He glances up when we walk in, his eyes locking with mine for a second.

"Find a dress?" he asks, not looking away from the mural.

I nod, "brought you some dinner," I say quietly, handing him a takeout box. "Figured you'd be hungry."

"Thank you," he says, opening the box and chowing down on the deli sandwich.

I climb back onto my stool and pick up my brush. There is a lot of work to be done.

"Is your family coming this weekend?" he asks.

I nod, "probably just my parents and Jules," I finish.

"No Jason?" he asks.

I look down at the floor and shake my head slowly, "We got into it over Thanksgiving, so I wouldn't be surprised if he didn't show."

"Oh…" he pauses, "about what?" he says cautiously.

"Everything that happened with you know who," I say.

"Why didn't you tell me?" he asks as he puts down his brush.

I shrug, "Not important."

"It is Sadie," he pauses, "but I'm sure he'll show up."

I shrug again and look away. "What about you?" I ask.

He turns and nods, "Yes, June is very excited to meet you guys," he finishes.

"I'm excited to meet her," I say. He just nods and turns back to our giant tree.

Levi and Tess refuse to let us see theirs until Saturday. The last time we saw it was over a month ago. I am really excited to see everyone else's paintings, too. We have all put so much work into these murals, and ourselves. Silence falls over us again. The sound of our bushes and the stools squeaking is enough to keep us motivated to keep going.

I sigh loudly, "I am beat."

He laughs and leans back, "Me too."

"Want to get takeout?" I ask, afraid of how he would respond.

He hesitates, "um-"

"With Tess and Levi, too," I interrupt him.

He nods, "Sure."

* * *

Derek and I go pick up some pizza and meet them back at my apartment. It's really obvious that we are all exhausted. Who knew painting could absolutely strip the life out of you?

I grab a slice off the coffee table and flop backward onto the couch. Derek sits on the floor in front of me, and everyone else is on the couch. "I could sleep for like 15 hours straight," I say.

Derek turns around and looks at me. "Nope, you can't. We have lots of work to do tomorrow," he says.

Tess laughs, "You are so serious about this," she says.

Derek laughs softly, "Okay, yes, but the winners get a

scholarship, and if we win, maybe it's my sign to go finish school," he says.

I had no idea he wanted to go back. He had told me before that he was nervous too because he's not the same person he was the first time he was at a university.

"Fair enough," Tess says, taking a bite of some cheesy bread.

We turn on another movie even though it is getting kind of late. I'm surprised they all didn't want to leave, but I think they were too tired to even get up. Halfway through the movie, I fall asleep. When I wake up, they were gone. Except Derek, who is also passed out on the other side of the couch.

I shake him awake, "Hey, it's late, we fell asleep," I say as he sits up.

He rubs his eyes, "Shoot, sorry."

"All good, I'm just going to go to bed," I say, getting up and locking my back door. "See you tomorrow," I say as he grabs his stuff and heads out the door.

He nods, "Goodnight."

I change into my pajamas and finish the movie I didn't even know we were watching. Maybe I should've just let Derek sleep there tonight and not have woken him up. I know he would rather sleep in his own bed than on my couch. Half of the decisions I make regarding him, I feel, are wrong, or I second-guess myself every time.

How in the world do I decide if telling him how I feel is the right thing to do?

31

~can you hear me?

D erek said we were only painting until 4:00 today. Which is fine by me. I could use a night to myself. I've fallen behind on my writing, reading, listening to music, and all my other hobbies. I do enjoy having friends to do things with, though, so I shouldn't complain. I'm okay with being pushed out of my comfort zone if it means getting my spark back.

But today, I'm telling him the truth. I have to. It's eating me alive inside, not telling him how I really feel. I'm full of doubt and confusion, but he deserves to know. Who knows what could really come of it?

Derek and I have similar clothing styles, I have noticed over the past few months. Sometimes we unintentionally match each other. Today is one of those days. He's wearing cream corduroy pants and a red long-sleeve shirt. I had thrown on my cream corduroy overalls at the last second and a brown long-sleeve shirt. With my brown Converse to utilize the sandwich method. His red shirt suits him well with his dark hair, and I like the color brown because it makes my hair pop.

"Do you think it's done?" I ask, stepping back to take it all in, every detail, every brush stroke.

He pauses and looks at it, "Just about. We'll take the next couple of days to clean it up and put the sealing stuff over it so preserve it," he says.

I nod and put my brushes away. "It looks really good, Derek."

"It does," he looks at me, "I'm proud of us, Sades, this wasn't easy." he smiles and inches closer to me.

"No, it was not," I say, slouching. "But we did it," I smile at him. Teeth and all.

"We did," he brings me in for a hug. He holds me for a minute and rests his chin on the top of my head.

He pulls away, "I think this program might have actually worked."

"You feel healed?" I ask, laughing.

"I am healeddd Sadieeee," he says in a loud bellowing voice. We laugh and put our things away.

"Alright, I'm heading out. I'll see you tomorrow, okay?" I say. I was going to tell him. But looking at our painting and all that we created, I just couldn't. I couldn't ruin this moment that we had worked on for four months. He deserves to just have this moment. After all, he's healing, too. We all were. I'm proud of us just for that.

"Sounds good, have a good night," he says, walking out the door.

I walk back to my room and meander onto my balcony. Even though it's cold, the fresh air is nice for my lungs. I make myself a cheap dinner with whatever is left in my fridge. Since I have to move out soon, I haven't bought any more groceries. After I finish eating, I click on Julia's contact.

She picks up after a couple of rings, "Hey, babe, what's up?"

"I'm going to go tell Derek how I feel," I say with no hesitation.

"Oh, you are?" she asks. I had already updated her on everything that went down on our ski trip, and she couldn't even fathom it.

"Yes, right now I think," I say. "Tell me it's the right choice," I say in a whiny tone.

"Sadie, just follow your heart because it is clearly leading you to Derek," she says. That hits me. She's very, very right.

"Okay, okay, I need to go get ready then," I say, getting up and going into my room.

"Okaayyy, let me know how it goes, you got this," she says.

I hang up and throw my phone onto my bed. I think I tried on about four or five different outfits and threw them all onto the ground. I don't want to try too hard, but I want to look put together. I decide on jeans and a cream sweater.

Hair and makeup are done. Subtle but definitely needed. I text Tess what I'm doing and tuck my phone into my pocket.

I can't believe I'm doing this.

I *love* him.

I love Derek Callahan.

I get off the elevator, rehearsing what I want to say in my head. Each version is different, so at this point I'm thinking about winging it.

I inch close to his apartment and take a deep breath. I knock softly on his door, and it creaks open. A cold wave rolls through my gut.

"Derek?" I call out quietly before I walk in. No answer. "Dereekkk?" I call out again in case he has his headset on. I step slowly inside, and the hardwood creaks under me. It's dark except for the light right above the island.

That's when I see him.

Collapsed against the island, half-sunk to the ground, his shoulders shaking. His other shoulder braced against the cabinet like he is being held together by a force.

Then I spot it.

The *knife* in his right hand.

My eyes widen, and I freeze. Everything in me is screaming to move. But I don't.

32

~still

It's strange what your brain does in moments like this. You think you would scream, or spring into action, or know exactly what to say or how to react. But instead, my brain goes numb. Everything slows down to a stop. Suddenly, I'm nineteen years old again, and the door slammed so hard against the wall that the picture frames fell and shattered into millions of shards of glass. I remember looking into his eyes, not seeing anything human left in them. I remember wanting the pain to stop. To have an ending. I remember how my heart tried to remain still even though it was finishing a race. I feel that again now. Like everything is spinning out of my control.

The terror and heartache are the same. But this time, *I'm not the one on the ground.*

"Derek!" I yell in a panic before realizing I need to be calm. He's weeping quietly, but he doesn't move an inch.

"Derek, it's me," I say in a calmer tone this time. "It's Sades," I continue. That sentence catches in my throat. He finally turns his head toward me slowly. His eyes are bloodshot red and glossed over with tears. He looks so tired. So gone.

I move toward him and slowly grab onto his shoulder. He stares at me. "I-I wasn't going to," his voice shakes. The words choke out of him as his hand with the knife shakes violently.

"I know, honey, I know. I'm here, just put the knife down," I say. I reach for it as his shaky hand reaches out with it for me to grab from his grasp. We are both kneeling on the ground facing one another. I carefully grab the knife, and it clatters on the hardwood behind me. I feel his head hit my shoulder, and his tears strike my sweater. And I realize, I have never seen him like this before. I don't say anything more because I don't know what to say. He's supposed to be the strong one. The steady one. Now he's breaking apart in front of me.

He quietly sobs, and I rub his back as we're still kneeling on the floor. I quickly look around to make sure there is no blood anywhere. I don't see any, and I breathe a sigh of relief. I got here in time. He pulls away and wipes away his tears with his sleeve.

"I'm really sorry, Sadie," he says in between sobs. He falls back into my shoulder.

"D it's okay, I promise. I'm not going anywhere," I say, trying to keep still.

"I don't want to die," he pauses. "I just want the pain to end," he says quietly, not looking at me. I clench my jaw and push my hair out from my face, trying to keep my tears from falling.

"I know you don't, it's okay," I say. I bite my lip to keep myself from losing it. I look around at his dark apartment. I don't move for a couple of minutes. Afraid he might break if I do. His crying slows, and he pulls himself off my shoulder and leans against the cabinet. His head falls back like he's been holding it up for too long. Why didn't he say he was hurting? I sit in front of him on the ground and wipe his tears from under his eyes and gently place my hand under his chin. He avoids eye contact with me and stares at the ground.

"I've got you, okay? I promise," I push his hair off his forehead. "Come on, let's get you to the couch," I say. He nods and quietly stands up. I watch his eyes lock with the knife. I grab his hand and lead him across the room. He falls onto the couch and rubs his eyes some more.

"I'll grab you some water quick, okay?" I say. He nods, and I run to the fridge to grab a bottle. I pick up the knife, put it back in the knife block, and set the block in the hallway. I walk back toward him. He looks exhausted.

"I'm good, Sadie," he says. I don't believe him. For once, I don't believe him when he says that.

"No, you're not, and that's okay," I respond and hand him the water.

"No, I'm good, really," he says as he takes a sip from the bottle.

I still don't believe him. "We'll just stay here tonight, okay?" I ask. He nods and lays his head in my lap.

"Did something happen?" I murmur. He flips onto his back with his head still in my lap.

He takes a deep breath, and it shakes on the exhale. "Not exactly. I was getting ready for bed and everything just felt so heavy, like my chest was being crushed." He responds, still slowly crying. I run my fingers through his beautiful chestnut hair slowly and look into his eyes. "I just wanted the noise to stop, just for a minute," he says, rubbing his bloodshot eyes.

"I know it's okay, you don't have to explain it all," I whisper. "You don't even have to make sense of all of it right now," I finish. He doesn't answer, just blinks up at the ceiling like he's trying to hold it together. "You're still you." His jaw clenches, and another tear rolls down.

"I'm so lost." His voice shakes. "I don't know what I'm doing anymore," he finishes.

I grab both his cheeks gently and say, "I know who you are. You are kind, caring, and thoughtful. You're the reason I've made it this far here." He grips the pocket of my sweats as if he didn't, I would slip away. "You're my best friend."

"I'm so tired, Sades," he admits. I can't hold it together anymore. My eyes water, and a tear runs down my cheek and lands on my shirt.

"I know D, but I have you. We have each other," The words get caught in my throat. He nods slightly and turns his head away from me. Nothing could describe the sting I am feeling in my chest. Like my heart wanted to fall out and give up. I have no idea what to do.

* * *

I turn on a movie to distract him from everything that is going through his head right now. He doesn't move from my lap, just turns his head toward the TV. For a while, I couldn't tell if he had fallen asleep, but I'm too scared to move either way. It's almost 10:00, and we haven't said anything for a while now. I just sit in silence watching the movie. I run my hands through his hair and carefully rub his back.

I'm tired and want to go to bed. But I'm scared to leave him alone.

"Derek," I whisper to see if he's sleeping. He doesn't respond. I lift his head and scoot out from under his head. I carefully place a pillow under his head and cover him with a blanket. I stand there for a minute trying to decide if I should go back to my apartment or stay here with him. After all, I did come here to tell him how I felt, but I obviously couldn't do that. As much as I want to get it off my chest. I decide to stay so he'd have someone here when he wakes up. I grab his pillow and blanket off his bed and make a makeshift bed next to the couch and TV on the floor. I leave the TV on for some noise and a little bit of light. I was hoping to spend the night here, but not like this.

* * *

I wake up on the floor to the smell of bacon and a little bit of burning. I slowly sit up and look into the kitchen. Derek is facing away from me, looking at the stove. I check my phone and it's already 9:00. I stand up, and he must've heard me get up because he spins around with a big smile on his face. Not exactly what I thought he'd be acting like after last night.

"Good morning, Sadie," he says with a smile.

"Morning... D.. "I rub my eyes. How are you?" I ask, walking into the kitchen.

"I'm good, you know you could've just stolen my bed last night instead of the hard floor," he says, using a spatula to scramble up some eggs.

I shrug and grab a piece of bacon off a plate, "It's okay, I didn't mind, wanted to stay close to you," I say firmly.

"I'm good, Sades, I promise, don't worry about me," he says, pouring the eggs onto the plate.

"I am worried about you, Derek," I say, looking into his eyes.

He pauses for a second, and his smile fades. "I know you are," he says quietly, looking at the ground, "and that scares me," he finishes and closes his eyes. I place my hand on his. I don't say anything, we just watch each other for a minute.

"I hate that you saw me like that," he pauses, "I really hate it," he finishes. I can tell he's holding back his tears.

"It's okay to show your emotions, it doesn't make you weak."

"I know, it just makes me feel like I don't deserve to have you as my friend," he says slowly.

Friend.

That word stings. But that's what we are. Because I haven't told him anything.

"I'm here, aren't I?" I ask quietly as I get close and wrap my arms around him. He wraps his arms around my upper back and rests his head on my shoulder. We stay there for a minute. Nowhere else we need to go.

He starts to pull away. "Wait, we didn't have plans last night. Why did you come to my room?" he asks, backing up to look in my eyes.

"Oh, um," I hesitate. It's noticeable. "Just thought I left something here," I say, grabbing the plate of eggs and shoving them into my mouth.

"Okay," he says with a smile. "You need coffee, get your stuff," he says, putting his plate in the sink.

"Agreed," I say, putting my dish away too. "Can we stop by my place first so I can change?" I ask, grabbing my things.

"Yes, and I can't believe you slept in jeans last night," he says, laughing. "You know where I keep my sweats."

I shrug and look down at my jeans. "Honestly, it wasn't that bad." I take a deep breath and tuck my hair behind my ears.

"Well, you deserve a coffee," he says as he opens the door.

"I can't say no to that," I say, walking out the door, and he follows close behind.

I really want to tell him how I feel. But I know I can't now. I don't know if I ever can.

33

~undone

I go back to my room quickly after we got coffee, but I insist that we should be working all day. I don't want to leave his side. He has to be tired of me asking him if he's okay. But I just don't believe him. I don't know what his exact intentions were last night, but I know what he used to struggle with. The main question I'm asking myself is, how in the world do I help? What in the world am I supposed to say? That part is beyond me.

What if I hadn't gone to his room in the first place? Who knows what would've happened? Maybe I would be visiting him at the hospital instead. Has he talked to his therapist yet? Do his parents know? Was this the first time since we've been here? I have so many questions to ask, but I can't.

I stare at him, adding some subtle details to the roots.

"What did you do after you dropped me off?" I ask, trying to sound subtle and not nosy.

"Just cleaned up from breakfast and was able to get in touch with my therapist," he says, not really looking up at me.

I breathe a sigh of relief, "Oh, that's good."

He nods slowly, "Yeah, but I have to start taking my meds again."

He stopped taking his meds? Why didn't he tell me?

"When did you stop?" I ask, trying not to pressure him.

He sighs and looks at me in my eyes. "About two months ago," he says as if he's embarrassed.

"Derek," I say and give him a look.

"I thought I was feeling better," he admits, "and when I realized that it was because of the meds, I honestly didn't know what to do," he says.

I nod slowly, "I get it."

"I think that's why I was lashing out," he says calmly. Like he's been here before.

"When did you lash out?" I ask.

"You know, at the ski lodge about you and Levi," he says casually.

I think back to that night. Everything he said and everything I wanted to say after. "Right."

"Yeah…" he pauses. "So just forget everything I had said, I wasn't in the right headspace."

I nod "okay," trying to hide the hurt in my voice. Did he not mean what he said? Does he really not want me anymore? Maybe I should just ask.

"I think we should talk about that-" I got cut off by Levi and Tess as they walk into our room. I had told Tess what happened, but told her not to bring it up. So they act normally.

"How's it coming in here?" she asks, sitting on one of our stools.

"Mediocre," Derek says and takes a deep breath. Tess shoots me a look, and I shrug. I'm starting to think the universe doesn't want me to tell him. But then again, our timing has always been bad.

Tess and Derek talk about our painting as I sit in the corner on my stool.

Levi steps closer to me from the entrance of the room, "Hey, how's it going?" he says, looking over my shoulder.

"Um, not bad," I say, turning around to face him. He's closer than I thought. I didn't tell Derek we weren't talking anymore, so I hope he's not getting any sort of idea.

He looks at me, "You look pretty," he says, almost under his breath.

"Levi," I gave him a look and raise my eyebrows.

"What I can't say, my friend is pretty?" he asks.

I roll my eyes and change the subject. "You guys ready for Saturday?"

He nods and twirls a brush around in his fingers. "I think so."

"I'm excited to see it," I say, looking up at him.

Tess turns to us, "Levi, let's go, we got work to do." he nods and walks away with her. "What was that about?" Derek asks.

If only he knew. I wish I could tell him.

Tell him how my stomach turns every time he walks in the room. How I smile every time he calls me Sades. How every time we painted, I had hoped he would kiss me. How when we were skiing, I wished he would hold my hand all the way down the hill. How if our pasts weren't sneaking up on us and getting in our way, we could be together by now.

I hesitate. "Nothing, just their painting," I smile and get back to work on deciding which finish to add on top of our painting. I thought we were almost done, but turns out there were a lot of little details to perfect. I get why Derek wants it to be perfect, though. It's one of the things we have total control of.

"I actually think I might implode," I announce, sitting on the ground in front of our mural.

"Me too," he sighs and stares at it. "Skippy's?"

"Yep," I say, standing up and grabbing my bag. He nods and follows me out the door. I slip my beanie and gloves on as we leave the building. We rush to Skippy's, and my teeth chatter the whole way. Even when we sit down in the usual booth.

Derek sips his water, "You didn't tell Levi, right?" he asks.

"What?" I reply.

"About last night," he says, looking at the table.

I shake my head, "No, Levi and I aren't talking like that anymore," I say. It just slipped out. I want to continue, but I feel like there isn't much else to say.

"Oh," he says, "why not?"

I shrug and grab my milkshake from the waitress, "better as friends, I guess," I say.

He nods slowly.

"Neither of us were ready." As soon as I say that, I realize how he could take it. That I'm not ready for a relationship at all. But that's not the truth. Not even close.

"I'm glad you're both prioritizing yourselves," he replies.

I nod, "Yeah, I think he's dealing with some stuff."

"Yeah, he is, that's why I was wondering if you told him. I don't want to make it worse for him."

"He'll always be there for you, D," I say, looking into his eyes.

He shrugs and starts to devour his burger. As do I. I normally don't get burgers, but once he ordered one, I wanted one too.

"You're crazy for not getting cheese on it," he laughs at me.

"I don't really like melted cheese," I say, and show him the rest of my burger.

"Anyways, when are you starting at SCSU?" he asks.

"Spring semester, so only a month or so," I say, smiling.

"Oh, that's good," he says, but his face tells a different story. I had thought a lot about this. After this weekend, we all go our separate ways. How am I supposed to get through my first semester back at college without my friends? I know I'll make other friends, but no one will ever come close to understanding me on the level that they do. But that's part of going back into the adult world. Figuring out how to be on your own and not rely on other people. But it was nice not to have to carry it all by myself for a while.

I could definitely use some alone time to recharge tonight, but I'm nervous to leave him alone. He says he's fine and that it was just a one-time thing and that he's taking care of it, but I already missed the signs once. I thought I knew him better than I knew anyone. That I would be able to see if he was struggling. But I couldn't. I didn't. I was so consumed in my own problems that I failed my best friend.

I failed him.

Now I need to fix that. But how?

* * *

He walks me back to my apartment, and I offer him to come in for a movie again. He just shrugs and plops down on my couch.

"Are you okay? Do you want something to drink?" I ask him gently.

He shakes his head and focuses on the movie. It's dark in my apartment. I took a bunch of my lights down and packed them up. The only light came from the glow of the TV. I sit next to him and pull a blanket over my knees. He grabs a corner of it and slowly leans his head onto my shoulder.

I feel him take a deep breath. "I'm really sorry," he says, voice cracking.

I don't move an inch, "for what?" I ask.

He doesn't respond right away. "Worrying you."

I tuck my hair behind my ear. "It's okay. I just want you to be okay," I say gently, looking at the TV screen.

He nods and doesn't say anything else. The lack of lights in my room is making me more tired than I already was.

I got up to get ready for bed. Pajamas on and makeup off. When I came back to the living room, Derek had fallen asleep on the couch. This time, I don't wake up. I grab the blanket and drape it over him. I flip the lock on my doors and leave my bedroom door slightly cracked just in case he needs something.

I hope he knows how much I care. How much I wish I could take away any pain he's feeling. I wonder if he can tell. If I have been a good enough friend to him, like he has been to me.

When I thought about falling in love again, I thought it would be electric all the time. Not full of sorrow and dismay. I hope it's just temporary, and soon we can feel the electricity again. For each other, and for ourselves.

34

~rooted

A snowstorm blew in this morning. It's supposed to last all night. The wind is crazy. I could hear it from inside my apartment. Trees were blowing everywhere, and I could hardly see two feet in front of me. It's beautiful, though. It's the only kind of storm I'm not afraid of. Snow can't hurt me.

But today's the day.

Months of painting and preparation have brought us here. To the end. I'll be staying in New Haven, but everyone else will be leaving. Derek will probably go back to Boston. Levi and Tess go back to their homes. I'll be alone again.

I sit in my room trying to decide what to do with my hair. If it's worth it to curl it for it to get ruined in the wind and snow? It might be. I stare at my reflection in the mirror. I had already zipped up my new dress. The thought of wearing heels scares me in this weather, so my Doc Martens will have to do. I look down when my phone buzzes on the counter.

Derek: *ready for this?*

Me: *I think so...*

I smile as I start on my makeup. I watch my hand tremble as I grab my foundation brush. I don't know why I'm so nervous about this. I think I just want to prove to my family I'm not broken anymore. That I survived. As much as I still have healing left to do, I'm not the same girl as I was when I got here. Hollow-eyed, quiet, afraid to speak up or to even take up space in this world. Hopefully, I'll never be that girl again.

I hear a faint knock on my door. It's Derek. I'm ready. I'm ready for this. He's standing there in his brown suit that fits him just right. He has some product in his hair to make it look perfect and a little less shaggy than it normally is. But the messy hair suits him.

"Hey, you ready?" he asks as I turn around to grab my stuff. When I turn back to face him in the doorway, he smiles. "You look great," he says with his bright smile.

"So do you, Mr. Callahan." I step out and close the door behind us. We have to be there a few hours early to move the mural and set up in the gallery hall. I'm counting on Derek and Levi to move it because I have a feeling I won't be able to help much. We speed walk over since the wind is still blowing snow all around us. He offers up his arm as we walk through the snow so I don't slip. I take hold of his bicep and inch closer to him. When we finally make it in, we see the other two. Tess is wearing a silver sparkly dress. One that reminds me of what I would wear to Christmas Eve Church as a child. But it looks good on her. Her black hair and silver jewelry pull it all together.

When I look at Levi, he's already looking at me. He's matching Derek with a plain suit and a bow tie. His suit is black, though. His dirty blonde hair falls over his forehead, and he looks taller than usual.

217

Tess and I watch as they carry out our mural into the gallery. It's one of the first ones out there. Everyone else is still adding finishing touches. Then, we watch as they turn the corner with Tess and Levi's painting.

"Wow," I say, staring at it. I turn to Tess, and she's beaming at it.

"Do you like it?" she asks, all giddy.

I smile at her, "I love it."

She squeals and runs over to it. I watch the three of them look at it and point out things on it. Derek comes back over to our painting.

"Theirs looks so good," he says.

"I like ours best," I say, moving some of our stuff around. He laughs and fixes his hair. "You okay?" I ask. I keep replaying that night in my head. I know he isn't okay. But racking my brain for how to help isn't working anymore. I'm defeated. I can't tell him how I feel, and part of me wonders if the other night was my fault. He nods and gives me a smile. A smile, I can't tell if it's fake or not.

Our families get to come in at 6:00, along with anyone else who is interested in some random paintings. The scholarship people are coming as well. I think there is only one scholarship to be earned, though.

Just shy of 6:00, Derek is pacing anxiously, waiting for people to come in.

"Can I tell you something?" he says, looking over at me.

I nod, "of course," I say, thinking it'll be about the other night.

He takes a deep breath. "I also got into SCSU."

My jaw drops, "You what?!" I'm in complete shock. "When did you even apply?" I ask, getting closer to him.

"Before you did," he starts, "but I don't know if I'll go." He bites his nails and avoids eye contact.

I drop my shoulders. "Derek, you have to."

"I don't know if I'm ready, Sadie," he says, still pacing.

"I get that," I hesitate before continuing. "But I believe in you," I place my hand on his shoulder. Before he can say anything else, the door swings open and a ton of people file into the room. We both straighten up, and I rehearse in my head what to say when people ask about our painting.

A man in a beige suit and brown tie, in his mid-thirties, approaches us. "Hello, my name is Dr. Scott Joiner, I'm the owner of Yale University Art Gallery," he says promptly.

"My name is Sadie Harper," I say with a smile, extending my hand to shake his.

"My name is Derek Callahan," he says, shaking his hand too.

He looks our painting up and down. "Tell me a little bit about your painting," he says, finally cracking a small smile.

I take a deep breath to remember what we rehearsed. This could be all or nothing to convince Derek he should go back to college, just like I am. I look at Dr. Joiner right in the face, "We painted this tree to represent everything we've survived." I start by strongly gesturing to our tree. "The weathered bark, the deep roots, they show what we've been through. How we've stayed grounded, even when things got difficult," I say with a smile on my face.

Derek nods and looks at me, then back at Dr. Joiner. "Every ridge in the bark, every individual leaf is there on purpose. The leaves show different layers of healing like anger, grief, and hope," he finishes. I look at him proudly.

Dr. Joiner nods approvingly. I think he likes it. "Impressive," he says, walking away. "Nice to meet you both."

Derek gives me a reassuring nod and a smile. We both

breathe a sigh of relief as the next lady comes around and another man asks about our tree. We recite the same thing to them.

"My parents are here," Derek says, looking at the entrance. I've never seen him smile so big then when his little sister ran to him and he scooped her up in a hug.

He hugs his parents too, and they finally turn to me, "You must be Sadie," they say, getting closer to me. "We've heard so much about you," his mom says, hugging me tight. I look at Derek and raise an eyebrow at him. He talks about me? He shrugs and gives me his awkward smile. The one I missed so much.

"This is incredible, you two," his dad says, looking at our tree. Derek resembles his dad. Their dark hair and their smiles look almost identical.

"Thanks, Dad, we'll see you guys after in the lobby, okay?" he says, giving them their cue to go look at the other murals. I think he's just nervous in front of them. It seems to me they don't know what happened the other night. He should tell them.

I wait anxiously for my parents and Julia. Hopefully, they were able to make it through the blizzard. The road to get here can be daunting, especially when it's snowing. The curves and hills can make it really slippery. My dad has driven that road many times for work, and I know Julia rode with them, so that eases my anxiety.

We smile at anyone who comes across our mural. I catch Derek watching me every so often. I nervously pull the bottom of my dress down and fix my sleeves, waiting for my parents. After the first thirty minutes, I look at the door and finally see them walk in. I breathe a sigh of relief.

"They're here," I smile at Derek and point to the entrance. My parents and Julia spot us and wave. Trying to get around the immense number of people at the entrance. "Wait," I say as a man walks in behind them with his head down.

"Is that your brother?" Derek asks, looking in the same direction.

I smile, "he showed." I exhale, "he actually showed." I didn't think he would. Not after Thanksgiving. I didn't deserve for him to show up. He didn't need to. But for once, I feel like he cares about me again. Like he once did.

When we were in fourth and fifth grade, a boy shoved me on the playground. Jason came over and gave him a massive wedgie before telling on him. Afterwards, he gave me a hug and went back to his kickball game with his friends. When he found out about Chase, I played that day over and over again in my head. Wishing he would protect me again like he once did. But he didn't. That devastated me just as much as everything else did.

He just looks at me as they walked over. He smiles a very small smile. I look at him as they come up to us, and I don't hesitate to wrap my arms around him first. I don't let go for a while, and he holds the back of my head just like he did that day. The day he would've beat that kid up for me. I felt safe again. Something has changed in him. He doesn't have to say anything, but I can tell that now, he would do anything to protect me.

I finally let go and smile at my parents and Julia, "glad you guys made it." I'm smiling ear to ear.

Julia looks up at our tree, "This is incredible," she says.

I smile at her, "Thank you."

"Who knew my little sister was good at painting?" Jason says, looking at me, then to Derek.

I shrug, "I didn't know either," I say, cracking a small laugh.

I watch my dad watch me and put his arm around my mom. "I love it, buggy," he says, getting choked up. My dad is not one to cry either. The only time I have ever seen him shed a tear is when I woke up next to him in that hospital bed. Everyone cried that day.

I watch them walk away after I point out Tess and Levi. They wander over to see their beautiful depiction of the ocean. Not quite fair that Tess used to major in art. She had an advantage. But that doesn't make our tree any less special. They both have their own unique stories. Just like each of us.

35

~because of it

After an hour and a half of standing in front of our tree, Clara walks onto the small stage with a microphone. Everyone gathers and faces her except for us and the other painters. We stay by our paintings. "Today, we have a very special guest here to find one special painting to display in his Yale University Art Gallery. Please give a warm welcome to Dr. Scott Joiner," she says, smiling and gesturing to him as he walks on stage. We clap softly. I look over at Derek, who is not good at hiding when he's nervous.

"It'll be okay," I say, grabbing his arm. He just nods and watches the stage.

"Thank you." Dr. Joiner says quickly as the claps die down. "The following pair of painters whose mural I will be displaying are..." he pauses and looks around the room. I take a deep breath, knowing it isn't the end of the world if we don't win. Because we didn't come here for a scholarship or anything like that. We came here to heal. I watch as he brings the microphone back up to his mouth. "Sadie Harper and Derek Callahan, would you please come up here?" he says with a smile.

Oh my gosh. That's us.

I turn to Derek, and both of our jaws are on the ground. "Derek, we got it," I say, smiling so big.

He picks me up and twirls me around before setting me back down and locking eyes with me for what feels like forever. He awkwardly clears his throat, "Let's get up there," he smiles, and grabs my hand. I follow him up there, and Dr. Joiner presents us with a certificate for the scholarship for each of us.

I can't believe it. I genuinely can't believe it. I scan all the people in the audience, clapping for us and smiling. Even Tess, who I know, also deserved to win it.

Dr. Joiner gestures to the microphone for us to say something. Derek looks at me to go first.

"Thank you so much, Dr. Joiner. What an honor." I pause and look around. "A lot of us came here hopeless. Searching for meaning when we thought we had none," I continue. "Our tree back there represents that. It shows that we're still standing. Not despite everything, but *because* of it." I smile and hand the microphone to Derek.

He takes a deep breath before bringing it up to his face. "It's a depiction of our hardship and how we have come out the other side still standing, and full of beauty. We are grateful for the opportunity this program has given us to create something like this and to have it shown in your gallery," he looks at Dr. Joiner with hope in his eyes. "Thank you," he finishes. We both smile and look around at everyone in the audience. Everyone claps once more, and Derek brings me in for a hug. Even when the claps stop and people start to file out, he doesn't let go. One hand on my upper back and one on the back of my head. "I love you," I whisper in his ear. I didn't mean to. I swear it just

224

slipped out. I'm an idiot. Now is not the time to confess my feelings.

"I love you too, Sades," he whispers back. Or maybe it was.

My face erupts in a smile before he continues, "I couldn't have done this without my best friend."

I feel my heart stop for a moment, and my smile fades to nothing.

Best friend.

Right. I guess he doesn't love me like that. At least not anymore. I put the smile back on my face so he doesn't notice. This is a kind of ache I've never known.

We walk into the lobby together and look for our parents. They have somehow found each other and are talking. His dad to mine and my mom to his. We smile as we approach them. My parents pull me in for a hug, and so do his. When my parents finally let me go, Julia grabs me and squeezes me tight. "You're the best person I know," she whispers in my ear. "And I am so unbelievably proud of you."

I smile, "I love you, Jules." I reply.

I watch Jason stand further away. I look at him and smile. I grab him for another hug. "I'm sorry, Sadie," he starts, "I promise to never let anyone hurt you again." I don't say anything. "You have my word," he continues.

I nod and pull away. A tear rolls down my cheek. "I know," I say with confidence. Because this time I believe him.

"I'm so proud of how far you've come," he finishes. I look up at him. A tear falls from his eyes, too. "Love ya, punk," he says with a smile.

"Love you, jerk," I say, hugging him quickly once more. I can't be mad anymore. As much as I want to, and as much as I still need to move on. I know that life is too short to stay mad at the people you love. He's the only big brother I have. I need him as much as he needs me.

We turn back to our parents, who are just watching us. Derek has his arm around his sister, and he smiles at me.

"We have to go out to dinner to celebrate," my mom says, "all of us."

We all nod and find a place to go. Not Skippy's this time. This deserves something fancier.

I spot Levi and Tess on our way out of the building. I wave and blow kisses to them. They make hearts with their hands back. I text our group chat quickly to tell them we'll meet up later for our last night. I think about the time I had with Levi. How easy it was, simple. I liked it like that. But it wasn't real. It wasn't right. I gave up what I had with Levi because I knew it wasn't meant to be. He isn't who I'm supposed to be with.

I look at Derek as we make our way out of the building. "Are you going to go back to college now?" I say smiling.

He nods, "yeah," he pauses, "I think I will."

I ruffle his hair, "yay."

I tuck my hair behind my ears and try not to trip over everyone else leaving the building too. I catch a glimpse of Derek ahead of me with his parents, and it reassures me that even though Derek and I may never get the chance to be together, we'll always be in each other's lives. He will always be my best friend.

36

~snow lights

The nine of us walk into a dimly lit seafood restaurant. Derek's sister, June, taps me on my shoulder while we wait for our table. I turn to her with a smile, "Thank you for looking out for him," she says softly, so he can't hear.

I gently grab her shoulder, "always," I smile, and look toward Derek.

"He means everything to me," June continues. "And you mean everything to him," she finishes before running back to their parents. I don't move after she says that. I have never been more confused in my life.

We sit down, but I can hardly get a word in with this many people talking to one another. I sit next to Julia and Jason. Derek sits across from me with June. He's leaving tomorrow. I don't know if it'll ever be right to tell him. Will it even matter?

I'm glad to finally catch up with Jason. He has a girlfriend, but was afraid to tell me, but I'm happy for him. I'm excited to meet her.

"Hey, I need to tell you something," I whisper to Jason.

"Yeah?"

"Since Chase showed up and broke the restraining order, there will be a court date and he'll probably get jail time," I say, but shudder when I say his name. "I don't know exactly how it works, but hopefully for at least a couple of years."

He looks at me and smiles. "That's really good, I'm glad, Sades."

I nod vigorously, "me too."

Derek clears his throat and looks at me. He wants to tell both of our families about SCSU. "Sadie and I have some news," he says loud enough for everyone to hear.

"Are you guys finally dating?" Julia whispers in my ear.

I slap her arm, "No, we aren't," I say. But I can understand why she would think that, because why did he say it like that?

"What is it?" June says impatiently.

He takes a deep breath and looks toward me. I nod for him to go ahead. "We both are going to Southern Connecticut State in the Spring," he says with a big smile.

They all smile and cheer for us. "That's so awesome for you two," his mom says, reaching to hold his hand on the table.

"You will have the best time there," Jason says, giving me a side hug.

Derek smiles softly at me and continues to eat his crab cakes. I am beyond excited to go back to school and to still have a friendly face with me. Maybe eventually we'll find our way to admitting how we feel. Maybe eventually our timing will be right, and both of us can be happy. I can hope. But getting my hopes up won't help when my heart may just break in the end.

* * *

We pay the bill and start to leave the restaurant. Our dads go to pull the cars around. They're staying the night in the hotel nearby to help us move out tomorrow. I hug everyone, and I watch Derek hug June for a while.

It's snowing and the wind is blowing around us when we walk out of the building. It's dark, but the parking lot is lit by the street lights.

"Want to ride with me?" he asks as our families leave.

I nod, and I slip on my hat and gloves before we walk out from under the overhead of the building.

"Ready to run?" he asks playfully, hardly glancing at me. I nod and put my hood up too. "Here," he holds out his hand for mine. I just look at his hand. I don't move. He sticks it out even further toward me.

I breathe deep and take his hand in mine. "On three?" I ask, seeking out where his car is, but I don't see it.

He counts down from three, and we sprint across the parking lot. He doesn't let go of my hand. For the first time in a while, I hear him laugh. Like, actually laugh. We keep running without paying attention to where we're going and accidentally run past his car. He realizes before I do and jerks me backward, "It's right here!" he yells over the wind blowing in our ears.

"Oh shoot!" I yell back and turn around. He tries to open the doors, but the handle is covered in snow, so he can't on the first try. I stand right behind him. He turns to face me, "Of course it's locked!" he yells. I don't reply. I watch him turn back to the car and fumble with his keys unsuccessfully.

He turns back to me but doesn't say anything. His face is eight inches from mine. A large gust of wind blows a ton of snow off the hood of his car and onto us. We laugh, and he puts his arm around my back and pulls me in to protect me from all the snow.

229

His hood falls off. I can see all the individual snowflakes in his chestnut hair. I'm laughing so hard, my back hits the side of the car. He turns to stand in front of me. I've missed his laugh. I've missed him. He isn't trying to unlock his car anymore, just staring at me. I can feel the snowflakes on my eyelashes. I blink and feel some of them fall off.

Suddenly, he slips on the ice and uses one arm to catch himself against the car. Right above my right shoulder. I turn to look at his hand and back at him. I watch his foggy breath as he breathes out and smiles.

The wind cuts around us. He locks his eyes onto mine. His ocean blue eyes. His beautiful smile. His rosy cheeks from the cold. His lips I've wanted for so long. My stomach does a flip as he brings his other hand up to my chin and gently lifts it closer to his.

His thumb brushes just under my jaw, and I forget how to breathe.

"Tell me I'm not imagining this, Sades," he whispers, stepping closer.

I shake my head slowly, not breaking eye contact.

"Because I don't think I could take it if I were," he confesses.

I tilt my head just slightly, "You never were."

He lets out a breath, slow and shaky, his gaze drops to my lips, then back to my eyes. "If I kiss you now," he says, voice raw, "there's no going back." For a moment, neither of us moves.

A soft smile tugs at my lips, "We've waited long enough."

He nods before leaning in, slow and deliberate, giving me all the time in the world to stop him.

I don't.

37

~anchored

— Four Months Later —

I sling my guitar over my shoulder and venture out of my apartment. I go to the quad and look around at everyone lying out, trying to catch the first glimpse of the sun after a long winter. It's beautiful outside. The weather I've been waiting for with bated breath. I spot him sprawled out on a blanket. "Hi," I say, sitting next to him.

"Well, hi there, Sades," he says, gently pushing my hair behind my ear and looking into my eyes. I strum my guitar slowly, not losing eye contact. His plain white tee and jeans match my white tank top and jean skirt. Unintentionally, as always.

I sing my little tune, I've been working on that he's been telling me to record and put on the internet. I wouldn't dare do that. It's like my little hidden talent.

"You know when I knew I loved you?" he asks out of the blue.

My stomach flips, and I keep strumming softly, "Hmm,

231

when?"

He smiles, "I've loved you since the first night we went to Skippy's." he forces the hair out of his eyes and looks into mine.

My jaw slightly falls. "You loved me all that time?" I ask even though, looking back on our months there, I should've been able to tell. The late nights working on our tree. The movie nights. The walks. The dinners. The ski trip. Everything about it. I should have known. I should have listened to Tess and Jules. I was an idiot, not too.

"Yes, but I never wanted to rush you," he continues, "I knew that eventually we'd get our timing right." He leans in close to me.

I can feel my face getting red. "I think I always loved you, too. I just hadn't realized it, I was too scared," I say, picking at the grass around me. "That's why I came to your room that night, to tell you," I say, smiling. "I never even realized you wanted me," I finish.

"Sades, I've wanted you since the day I met you," he replies. His lips graze mine, and I stare into his eyes when he pulls away. We both just smile. It's hard to believe this hadn't come up until now. I guess we were just too consumed with one another and getting back into the swing of being in college.

He takes a breath, "I also want to let you know the new meds are working." He smiles and grabs my hand. "They've been helping."

"That's great, D," I say. "I'm proud of you."

He cocks his head to his left, "For what?"

"For taking care of yourself," I pause. "And for taking care of me," I run my hand through his hair.

He smiles softly, "I will always take care of you."

I put my guitar down at my side and take a bite of the sandwich he made me. Turkey with American cheese and mayo.

He grabs my hand. "Guess who I heard from today," he smirks.

I look at him in confusion, "Who?" I ask impatiently.

He smiles and places his hand gently on my knee. "Dr. Joiner."

I put my sandwich down and throw my hands up when he doesn't continue, "And?!"

He pauses, "It's ready," he says with a smile.

I clap my hands and start to pack everything up. "Let's go then," I smile at him. His teeth shimmer in the reflection of the sun. They distract me. I grab his hand as we walk back to my apartment. I stare at the SCSU sign as we walk. I can't believe this is real. I'm about to finish my first semester back at school, and I did it. I am myself again.

Yale University Art Gallery is a short drive from campus. I wear a green sundress with some strappy sandals. It's finally almost summer. Derek wears a green button-up and some jeans. This time, the matching is intentional. He turns to smile at me as the building comes into view.

"We're here to see our painting," he says as we walk up to the front counter. He gives them our names, and I nervously squeeze his hand. She gestures for us to follow her, so we do. Down one hall, then another, and another. This art gallery is huge. Countless beautiful paintings hang on the walls. Sculptures and photographs, too. Finally, we reach a hall of murals. They're all as big as ours.

"It's at the end here," the receptionist says. I smile at Derek and skip to follow her. I can't even contain myself.

There it is. Our tree. Weathered and tired as ever, but still standing.

Just like us.

I cover my mouth in shock. "This is not real life," I say, staring at it in awe. I jump up and down ecstatically.

"Want me to take your picture in front of it?" she asks. I nod enthusiastically and hand her my phone. He wraps his arm around my waist and pulls me in close. We smile so big for the picture. Our outfits even match the tree. Our tree.

We admire it some more, and Derek doesn't say much. Just exchanged glances between me and the tree, "we did that, Sades," he says, rubbing my back. He kisses my forehead gently. "We really did that."

* * *

"We saw our tree in the gallery today," I say, slipping into the all-familiar red booth that is Skippy's diner.

"Love that for you guys," Tess says, shoving a straw into her strawberry milkshake.

"Where's Mr. Levi?" Derek asks, looking at Tess.

"Right here," he says, scooching next to Tess in the booth. I swear he came out of nowhere. That's what he does best.

I look at him and his unfamiliar tennis shoes. "Wait, where are your boots?" I ask him.

He sighs and drops his head back, "My girlfriend says I should branch out," he says hesitantly.

Tess almost spits out her milkshake. "Girlfriend? You finally asked her out?" she asks.

He nods, "Yeah, last week, sorry forgot to bring it up," he laughs.

We all roll our eyes, and Derek grins and reaches over for a fist-bump. "Good for you, man," he says.

We order our food and catch up some more. Tess went on a two-week backpacking trip to a bunch of national parks with her ex-boyfriend, who she became friends with again. Muddy territory, but she'll do what's best for her. I believe that.

Derek turns and whispers in my ear, "I'm glad you're mine." he smiles.

I can feel the color rise in my face, and I sip on my latte. "Me too," I whisper back.

No one really prepares you for what it's like to say goodbye to a season of your life you hated and loved at the same time. A season of growth, setbacks, love, grief, terror, and hope that the future will be better. It's strange how it can feel like an ending and a beginning at the same time. I've become a better version of myself. Maybe stronger. Maybe just someone who's still trying to heal and move on.

It's difficult to explain who I am now. But I'm getting closer. We hugged goodbye. We promised we'd visit one another. Because we mattered. Our journey and victories mattered.

The thing no one tells you is that moving forward doesn't always feel like victory. Sometimes, it's like leaving behind a version of yourself you're not sure you'll ever meet again. That is perfectly okay with me. Because forward is still forward. You can always get better. Stronger. Braver. Happier.

If you just keep moving *forward*.

About the Author

Carly Smith is a Minnesota-based author who fell in love with storytelling as a young girl. Her creative spirit has always guided her, and she's currently completing her B.S. in Communication with a minor in Writing. When she's not writing, you can find her curled up with a good book, behind her camera, or discovering new music. This is her debut novel, and she's grateful to anyone holding it in their hands.

You can connect with me on:

🖉 https://www.instagram.com/carly.smith11

www.ingramcontent.com/pod-product-compliance
Lightning Source LLC
Chambersburg PA
CBHW050308110726
47899CB00007B/2152